W9-BFM-567

Vow of Silence

DAYBREAK MYSTERY

B·J·HOFF

ACCENT BOOKS
CHARIOT FAMILY PUBLISHING
A DIVISION OF DAVID C. COOK PUBLISHING CO.

Accent Books™ is an imprint of David C. Cook Publishing Co.
David C. Cook Publishing Co., Elgin, Illinois 60120
David C. Cook Publishing Co., Weston, Ontario
Nova Distribution Ltd., Newton Abbot, England

VOW OF SILENCE
©1988 by B.J. Hoff

Cover design by Koechel/Peterson & Associates
First Printing, 1988
Printed in the United States of America
96 95 94 93 92 7 6 5 4 3

Library of Congress Catalog Card Number 87-72778
ISBN 0-7814-0528-9

FOR DANA AND JESSIE

Answered Prayers
And Dreams Fulfilled—
Gifts of Love Forever

A Voice is heard within the quiet spirit,
A Word comes in the silence to impart
The promise of a loving Father's care
And faithful keeping
Of the soul with a surrendered, trusting heart . . .

B.J. Hoff
From *Gifts to the Giver*

Prologue

The room was dim and drafty. The man's hands chilled as he spread out the silk-textured clown suit on top of the bed with meticulous care. First, the baggy white pants, then the oversized tunic—white on the left side, black on the right, topped by a frilly white ruff. Smoothing both pieces and draping them just so, he stepped back to consider the overall effect.

Satisfied, he reached into the open suitcase at the foot of the bed and took out a black skullcap and a pair of white gloves. After laying the gloves on top of the tunic, he examined the small black cap for a moment, twirling the *coif* on the tip of his index finger a few times before placing it just above the white ruffled neck of the tunic. Fishing a stick of gum from his pocket, he tucked it inside his mouth and began to chew.

Glancing down at a pair of plain black shoes sitting neatly beside the bed, he moved to check the contents of the suitcase one more time. Reassured that the second *Pierrot* suit, identical to the one laid out on the bed, was still folded in place beneath the few pieces of clothing he'd packed, he closed the lid and locked the suitcase.

Straightening, he glanced around the room until he spied a red plastic makeup kit on a slatback chair near the door. He went to get it, bringing it back and placing it neatly in line with the other items on the bed.

Once more he appraised the costume and its accessories, finally nodding with silent approval. A thought struck him, and he pulled his wallet from the back pocket of his jeans, sliding a photograph out from behind the lining of the bill compartment.

The only light in the room was a weak slice of afternoon gray filtering through a solitary window. He had to hold the photo close, at eye level, in order to see it clearly.

Enormous smoke-blue eyes gazed out at him above a smile touched with shyness and a distinct hint of mischief. Silver-blonde hair fluffed randomly about a heart-shaped face that was part gamin, part princess. It was an incredibly lovely face, wistful yet radiantly alive, unaware of its subtle, haunting beauty.

Moments passed as his gaze searched the eyes in the picture. He looked away as an unexpected gust of wind rattled the narrow windowpane. Looking back at the photo in his hand, he felt a smile begin inside him that spread slowly across his face.

The smile widened as his eyes left the photograph to glance at the clown suit on the bed. "I hope you're bright enough to appreciate the irony in all this, Whitney-love: the silent clown about to invade your silent world."

The smile fled, and he pressed his lips into a tight line. Picking up the makeup kit from the bed, he took it and the picture with him into the next room where there were two windows and more light. He crossed to a square wooden table, rough with peeling paint, on which he had earlier placed a swivel makeup mirror. Pulling up a chair, he sat down, scooting in close. For a moment he scrutinized his reflection in the mirror. Satisfied that he didn't need a shave, he carefully tucked the photo into a corner of the mirror and folded his hands on top of the table.

"So I've finally found you, Whitney-love," he said conversationally, wringing his smooth, well-manicured hands until his knuckles turned white.

Abruptly, he pulled one hand free and leaned forward to trace the outline of the face in the picture. "I've planned

8

something very special for you, little girl. Not like the others. This is going to be quite a performance. The best yet."

His eyes scanned the room. "Everything's ready for you. Planned, prepared, waiting. Just for you, Whitney-love."

A bundle of rope and a coil of wire lay side by side at the other end of the table; only inches away was a .38 revolver. A length of chain was wrapped loosely around the back of the chair across from him.

He leaned a little closer to the photograph. Pressing his finger hard against the surface of the picture, he began to jab at it repeatedly until the mirror toppled. Its crash shattered the silence of the room.

He pushed away from the table, his chair screeching on the wooden floorboards as he jumped up. The picture had fallen free from the mirror. He yanked it off the table and flung it angrily to the floor.

He stood unmoving, his breathing quick and ragged as he stared down at the photo. "It's payback time, Whitney-love. And you've got a lot of paying to do, little girl. A lot of paying."

He spat upon the picture, then slowly and deliberately began to grind it under the heel of his boot, digging at it over and over again until it crumbled beneath his foot.

1

Jennifer snuggled as close as she could to Daniel's large, solid warmth, secretly wishing she had heeded his advice to wear a heavy parka instead of her lighter stadium jacket.

The evening was frigid, but Daniel had been right: Shepherd Valley residents didn't pass up their favorite street festival for anything as insignificant as falling temperatures. They simply bundled up and huddled a little closer together to enjoy the fun.

Spying a small lath art booth on the other side of the street, she tugged at her husband's arm. "Wait, Daniel, there's a display over here I want to see."

Daniel gave Sunny, his golden retriever guide dog, a short command, and allowed Jennifer to lead him to the booth across the street.

"Oh, Daniel, I wish you could see this! It's absolutely beautiful." Jennifer admired the country scene in silence for a moment, then clasped her husband's hand and carefully placed it over the center of the picture. "It's a farm. It even has a wire fence and a windmill."

Skimming his fingertips over the three dimensional picture, Daniel nodded. "The barn, right?" He smiled as he traced the outline of the building.

"Yes. Here, feel right here, above the barn door. It's a hay loft."

"What's this?" He frowned, brushing his fingers from corner to corner over the upper area of the picture.

"Snow!" she told him delightedly. "And it looks so real, you can almost feel it falling on your face! Oh, Daniel, do you think we could buy it for the house? It would be perfect—a barn for our barn!"

Years ago, Daniel had remodeled an early American barn into a stunning, unique home that had eventually become a community landmark and conversation piece. Early in their engagement he had offered to buy a more traditional house for them, but Jennifer wouldn't hear of it.

"How much?" he asked skeptically.

"How much?"

"For the picture."

"Oh—yes. The picture." She hesitated.

One dark brow lifted. "That much, huh?"

"It *is* art, Daniel. Genuine art isn't cheap, you know."

The other brow went up. "Give me a hint."

"You could take it out of my salary."

"You're already in the red, kid. How much?"

"My Christmas bonus?"

"A bonus wasn't included in your contract, Jennifer."

"Neither was marriage to the boss."

"That's called a fringe benefit, darlin'." He stroked one side of his heavy dark beard, flashed a sudden smile in her direction, and said thoughtfully, "I suppose we could work out a deal on the picture, if it means that much to you."

Her hopeful expression slanted to narrow-eyed suspicion. "What kind of a deal?"

"You know that Piney Ridge brunch next month? The one that's being given to honor the winners of the state economics essay contest?"

"Uh-uh," she said firmly, crossing her arms over her chest. "No way. Definitely not."

"Honey, you'd enjoy it. They're having bagels and veggies—I know how you love your veggies—and no more than a dozen or so speeches." He paused. "I agreed to have the station cover it."

"Fine. I'll drop you off and pick you up when it's over."

"Oh, *I* can't go, Jennifer. Didn't I tell you? The brunch is the same day as the church's pancake breakfast. Gabe and I are already committed to the meal at the church."

She rolled her eyes at nobody in particular.

"The thing is, *somebody* has to go to Piney Ridge. I promised," he said virtuously.

"You know, I don't think I want this picture after all. Actually, I believe the barn is a little crooked. And the hay is definitely going to seed." She watched him carefully.

He shrugged. "Too bad, darlin'. It could have been yours."

"Oh, all *right!* I'll go to the brunch. But there's no one in the booth, Daniel. What if someone else buys the picture before we come back for it?"

"Don't worry, you can still go to the brunch," he said, taking her arm. "A deal's a deal."

She tried to clip him on the ankle, but he hugged her hard against his side, laughing. "Where are we supposed to meet Whitney?"

"At the high school concession stand. I think we're headed in that direction now."

Jennifer began to scan the crowd for a sign of Whitney, but the petite new director of the Friend-to-Friend Association was too small to spot easily among so many people.

With Sunny guiding Daniel flawlessly along the congested street, they walked on, occasionally slowing down to exchange greetings with friends or browse an exhibit. In spite of the cold, a carnival-like mood prevailed. As Jennifer had explained to Whitney earlier in the day, the festival was not only an annual reminder of the town's heritage, but it also served as a last lighthearted fling before the arrival of another mountain winter.

The entire downtown area had been cordoned off. Hundreds of people poured through the streets, milling about in large and small groups. A mixed chorus of laughter bounced from sidewalk to sidewalk, and a pungent blend of food aromas spiced the air. Music was everywhere; folk singers, school bands, and a variety of ethnic ensembles had staked a claim on almost every unoccupied square of ground. Clowns, some with drums, others with balloons and flowers, scampered in and out among the people. Turn-of-the-century, ivy-covered buildings gazed stoically down on arts and crafts booths, while dignified stone office structures shared their space with cotton candy trailers and popcorn stands.

Glancing up at Daniel, Jennifer saw that he was wearing his soft smile of contentment, the expression that meant he was enjoying himself immensely. In a warm rush of love for the big, gentle man beside her, she tightened her hand on his forearm. Still smiling, he freed his arm to drape it around her shoulder.

"You haven't seen Jason anywhere, have you?" he asked. Their nine-year-old son, adopted shortly after their marriage, was being treated to an entire evening at the festival by his Aunt Lyss and Uncle Gabe.

"Not yet. If I know our boy, he's pigging out with Gabe at one of the junk food stands," Jennifer said dryly. "I'm glad he's spending the night with *them*. Lyss handles tummy aches much better than I—" she stopped, pressing his arm. "There's Whitney. This way, Daniel—over here to your right."

Waving, Jennifer tried to get Whitney's attention, but the small, fair-haired young woman was watching Beulah Wilson whittle oak split ribs for one of her custom-woven baskets. Jennifer started to call out, then scowled at her own forgetfulness.

As they approached, she wondered, not for the first time,

what exactly it was about Whitney Sharyn that sparked an instinctive need to protect her.

It wasn't her deafness. Jennifer had sensed from their first meeting that Whitney, like Daniel, had accepted the limitations of her handicap and had gone on to make a quality life for herself. It was a life that was rich and productive, marked by an active Christian faith and a natural zest for living.

Unlike Daniel, however, who had been blinded only a few years earlier in an automobile accident, Whitney had lived with her disability from the time she was five-years-old. A particularly virulent attack of meningitis had totally destroyed her hearing.

Being deaf hadn't hindered Whitney's career, though. She amazed Jennifer with her sharp organizational skills, her smooth efficiency in directing the entire program of their mutual assistance organization for the handicapped, and her unconditional love and concern for other people.

Still, Jennifer sensed a sadness about the remarkable Whitney Sharyn that puzzled her. When first hired for the directorship, Whitney had revealed little in the way of personal information, only those facts required by the employment application. Even now, three months later, her background remained shrouded in mystery.

Although Daniel often accused her of trying to "mother" her new friend, Jennifer disagreed. She thought her protective attitude toward Whitney was more a response to the faint aura of vulnerability that seemed to hover about the young deaf woman. Jennifer strongly suspected that Whitney had been badly hurt, either physically or emotionally. There were subtle but unmistakable signs, she thought, that Whitney Sharyn had survived some manner of excruciating ordeal. Survived, but not without scars.

There were little things, she insisted to Daniel, that simply weren't right. Somewhere behind those enormous smoke-

15

blue eyes she was sure an old sorrow burned, a grief that continued to simmer. The quiet, gentle mannerisms; the odd, winsome smile; the mature, serene air of assurance were all touched with a hint of sadness.

Jennifer was convinced that Whitney lived with something that refused to give her peace. Whatever it was, it caused her pain. And although Jennifer found it impossible to explain, even to Daniel, she didn't so much feel a need to *mother* Whitney as she did to *heal* her. If only she could . . . .

Her thoughts drifted off when she saw Whitney turn in their direction and smile.

"I've been . . . looking for you," Whitney said as they approached. Her faltering but precise speech was accompanied by sign language.

Whitney's speech was slow, with an occasional stammer, but clear and remarkably distinct for one who had been deaf since early childhood. Two of the few things Jennifer *did* know were that Whitney was a graduate of the world's only liberal arts college for the deaf—Gallaudet in Washington, D.C.—and had taught at a Louisville school for the deaf almost four years before moving to Shepherd Valley. Although an expert lip-reader and fluent in verbal speech, her years of teaching in sign language had stayed with her; she often signed as she spoke.

"Where's Jason?" she asked.

"With Gabe and Lyss," Jennifer said, facing her to mouth the words carefully. "He's staying overnight with them after the festival."

"There goes my . . . partner for the rides," Whitney said with a small pout. Her face brightened at the sight of an approaching company of clowns. "Look, Jennifer!" she exclaimed. "Look at the little tramp!"

A diminutive hobo clown in front of the others was studiously pulling enormous plastic flowers out of a friend's ear. The expression of bewildered surprise on his painted

16

face sharpened with each blossom he retrieved. Spying the attentive Whitney, he raced up, bowed dramatically, and presented her with an oversize daisy.

Two of the other clowns hurried up, bumping their comrade out of place in their eagerness to offer Whitney the contents of their pockets. Laughing, she lifted both hands in protest at their antics, good-naturedly refusing their gifts of tissue carnations and colored bandanas.

"What's going on?" Daniel asked, shifting his weight beside Jennifer.

"Hm?" She glanced up at him. "Oh, sorry, darling. Whitney seems to have captured an entire circus of clowns. They're trying to outdo each other for her benefit. Oh, there's one of those—I can't think what you call them—the ones that wear the black and white tunics and the little black caps."

"A *Pierrot?*" Daniel offered.

"That's it. My dad calls them 'classy clowns'."

She watched as the *Pierrot* scampered up to Whitney and began to pantomime in a bid for her attention.

It occurred to Jennifer that the mime was a little too big to be as graceful as he obviously believed himself to be. *His makeup needs work, too,* she thought. The clown white on his face looked like it had been spray-painted on. It was even leaking into the small tufts of hair that peeped out from under his black, round skull cap. His wide red mouth was decidedly crooked, and the black paint outlining his eyes looked like it had been applied in a terrible rush.

When the *Pierrot*'s glance flicked away from Whitney to Jennifer for an instant, she felt an unexpected tingling of unease. The mime simply wasn't . . . *clownish,* she decided.

It was a ridiculous thought, but something about him reminded her of a face she'd once seen on the cover of a cheap horror novel in the supermarket. The clown on the book had been more frightening than funny. She had quickly turned away, unsettled by the nasty, grinning image. Something about the *Pierrot* now staring at her made her feel exactly the same way.

Shivering, she shook her head at her own foolishness and watched Whitney, who was still smiling at the clown. He performed another brief pantomime, then bowed in a fawning, dramatic manner. Immediately, he glided into a fluid, slow-motion routine which Whitney obviously found enthralling.

Losing interest, Jennifer turned to Daniel and Sunny. Daniel, apparently attracted to the sound of music nearby, had moved to stand just inside the oval lawn, listening to two young men play a fiddle and a dulcimer.

Jennifer glanced back at Whitney. Seeing that her attention was still focused on the clown, she went to join Daniel.

He was smiling and tapping his foot to the beat of the music while Sunny sat contentedly beside him, her head cocked with interest. Jennifer recognized the two musicians, twin brothers who attended the same church as she and Daniel; they often entertained at local events. Flame-haired and fully bearded, one was playing a sparkling hammered dulcimer accompaniment to his darker-haired brother's frenzied fiddle.

A vague, burning sensation squeezing her chest reminded Jennifer that she hadn't eaten since late morning.

"I could do with some food, Daniel," she said, taking his arm. "I'm sure I can't make it around the block without an infusion of at least two thousand calories."

"Name your poison, darlin'."

She wrinkled her nose. "Poor choice of words." She looked around. Seeing a concession stand only a few feet away, she tugged at his arm. "C'mon, Daniel—I smell chili dogs."

He groaned. "I had a hot dog for lunch."

"Whose fault is that? I offered to share my yogurt and peaches."

He grimaced. "Baby food."

"It's good for your skin."

"Most babies are red and wrinkled."

"Only the ones who don't eat their yogurt and peaches." Again she pulled at him. "I think I'll have *two* chili dogs."

With a sigh, he gave Sunny her forward command and they started off. "Where's Whitney?"

"She's still watching the clowns. The mime was treating her to a private performance," she explained as they crossed the lawn. "She's right over . . . "

Jennifer craned her neck to find Whitney in the crowd milling around the clowns. Slowing her pace, she pressed Daniel's forearm with her hand. He adjusted his stride to hers, asking, "What's wrong?"

"She *was* right over here." Jennifer stopped a few feet away from the corner where Whitney had been standing only moments before. At least twenty people were clustered around the sidewalk, watching the clowns do a series of acrobatic routines. Whitney was nowhere in sight, nor was there any sign of the *Pierrot*.

With some effort, Jennifer dismissed the faint touch of unease at the back of her mind. "That's odd. They were right here."

"They?"

"I told you, Daniel, she was watching one of those clowns." Anxiously, she continued to scan the crowd.

No Whitney.

She tried to swallow, but her mouth had gone suddenly dry. "Daniel, I can't find her."

"She probably went looking for a snack."

"No, we had planned to eat together. Besides," she added

19

tightly, "Whitney doesn't like being alone in a crowd like this anymore than you do."

As if he'd only then heard the concern in her voice, Daniel frowned. "She's probably right around the corner." He paused, then said gently, "Jennifer, Whitney is a grown woman. You don't have to stand guard over her."

Looking at him, Jennifer admitted to herself that most likely she *was* over-reacting. Still, there had been that feeling of distaste when the *Pierrot* had looked at her.

"It's just that she can't hear, Daniel—"

"And I can't see," he countered evenly. "But I don't necessarily need a keeper. And neither," he said pointedly, "does Whitney."

"I suppose you're right," she said, peering into the crowd and fervently wishing she hadn't left Whitney alone.

Whitney isn't *alone,* she silently reassured herself. How could anyone be alone when surrounded by hundreds of people in the middle of the street?

"Come on," Daniel said, as if he were aware that Jennifer's silence didn't necessarily mean acceptance. "We'll walk around and see if we can find her."

At first Whitney didn't realize how much distance she had placed between herself and the Kaines. Amused with the *Pierrot*'s playful charm, she watched him, laughing as he bowed, strutted and scampered, stopping every few seconds to make an exaggerated bid for her approval.

When it occurred to her that she was actually moving along the sidewalk with him, she stopped, glanced around, and turned to go back. Seeing her hesitate, the mime pranced up to her, raising his hand to get her attention, then pointing to something just over the heads of a couple strolling in front of them. Abruptly, he darted past the man and woman, motioning for Whitney to follow.

Uncertain but curious, Whitney hurried by the middle-

20

aged couple just ahead. The *Pierrot* turned and, seeing her, pointed across the street and up the block, in the direction of the Mountain Savings Building. Stepping off the curb, he smoothly threaded his way through the people thronging the blocked-off street and began jogging toward the bank building.

It took Whitney longer to clear the crowd. When she finally caught up with him, he was waiting, his face framed between white-gloved hands. Immediately he began to bob up and down as if he could scarcely contain his excitement.

Growing impatient, Whitney started to step up onto the high curb. The clown reached to take her hand, but she drew back so sharply, she lost her balance and nearly fell.

Her smile faded, and her face grew hot with a sudden tingling of unease. There were no booths or exhibits on this side of the street, which was one of the two exits from the festival. It was also completely dark now, and although the lighting was adequate across the street, on this side it was dim, shadowed, and distorted by the large buildings hovering over the asphalt. The only people close-by were few and scattered. Most of them were much farther up the block, heading toward the exit.

The clown saw her hesitation and immediately dropped his hand, giving her a puzzled look.

Annoyed with herself, Whitney shook her head as if to banish what she knew to be an irrational fear. She was being foolish. She was in the middle of a downtown street festival, surrounded by people and activity. She was safe.

Forcing a smile, but keeping her hands at her sides, she stepped up onto the curb. The mime's expression cleared. He hugged his arms to his chest as if he were overwhelmingly happy, then took a few more steps backward, stopping when he reached the corner wall of the bank.

A narrow alley dissected the block, bordered on one side by the weathered stone bank building and on the other by a shoe store. Shuffling excitedly from one foot to the other, the *Pierrot* pointed upward, to the roof of the bank.

Whitney frowned, her gaze following the direction in which he was pointing. At her uncertain frown, the clown scurried away from the front of the building, stepping just inside the narrow alley that ran between the bank and the shoe store. Indicating that Whitney should pay attention, he again gestured for her to look at the very top of the building.

Whitney walked over to where he was standing, letting her head fall back as she strained to see the roof.

The sky began to spin as she suddenly felt herself hauled backward. She had no time to react. Her feet went out from under her, and a white-gloved hand covered her mouth. At the same time, her arm was wrenched hard behind her back. The clown began to drag her roughly down the deserted alley, away from the lights of the festival, away from any help.

Terror roared through Whitney, overwhelming her, disorienting her as she was hurtled down the alley at an incredible speed. His hand on her mouth was a vise, mercilessly silencing her; her arm felt as if it would rip free of her shoulder any instant.

Nearly wild with fear and dazed with pain, Whitney's mind attempted to snap shut. Memories of the other time, the brutal, crazed violence that had been unleashed upon her, came crashing full-force against the present horror, and she felt the first nauseous pang of unconsciousness clutch at her.

Fighting for control, she stiffened in an effort to slow his momentum. She tried to yank her arm free, twisting in his arms, biting at the gloved hand across her mouth.

Behind her, he faltered. Seemingly thrown off balance by the strength of her resistance, his hand slipped, momentarily freeing her mouth.

Hot tears of helplessness scalded Whitney's eyes as she tried to scream, desperately forcing the sound up and forward out of her throat. Unheard and unmeasured by her deaf ears, she could still sense the weakness of her voice.

Praying someone would be close enough to hear her cries for help, she screamed again.

Enraged, her abductor swung her around to face him with such violence she thought her neck would snap. The painted white face glowering furiously down at her was no longer the face of a clown but, instead, a savage mask of evil. The black rim around the eyes was smeared, the red mouth a bloody slash of rage. Panic seized Whitney by the throat as she stared into the diabolical white face. She looked into his eyes and saw the glittering stare of madness blazing out at her.

She managed to bleat out one more weak cry just before the *Pierrot*'s hand lifted, then descended in a vicious chopping motion.

Nearly blind with pain, her last thought was a feeble, incoherent protest that this couldn't be happening again. But in that instant, she knew her most terrifying nightmare had become reality.

2

"She wouldn't have come this way," Jennifer said worriedly. "There's nothing over here but the exit." Holding on to Daniel's arm, she waited for him and Sunny to start across the street.

"We've come this far," Daniel said, stepping off the curb. "Let's go on down the block. If we don't find her, we'll go back to the oval and wait there."

It was darker on this side of the street and nearly deserted, except for the far end of the block, where a few people were passing between the sawhorses that had been set up as blockades.

"You think I'm being foolish, don't you?" Jennifer glanced up at him, anticipating his reply.

His answer surprised her. "No, I have to admit it's not like Whitney to just wander off without saying anything. Not for this long, anyway."

There's something wrong... I know it, I can feel it. Jennifer wavered between her growing anxiety and the need to convince herself she *was* overreacting.

They passed the dark glass storefront of the office supply center, then Kellerman's Pharmacy which was still open. With the amber glow of the streetlight now behind them and only faint, scattered shots of light from the festival to break the darkness, the street was deeply shadowed. She felt a peculiar sense of relief when another couple crossed from the opposite side and began walking in front of them, in the direction of the exit just ahead. Somehow, the sight of other people nearby helped to ease her apprehension.

"I suppose we might as well go back. There's no sign of her." In spite of her words, though, Jennifer continued to scan their surroundings. Something jabbed at her mind—instinct or fear, she couldn't be sure which. The memory of Whitney standing on the corner, innocently watching that clown, nagged at her relentlessly.

"Daniel, what if we can't find her? What if—"

Her words faded in the wake of two cries that came exploding out of the darkness, shattering the quiet of the night. A muffled scream from the direction of the alley just ahead collided with the startled outcry from the well-dressed woman in front of them.

Everyone stopped walking at the same time. Sunny began to strain on her harness, barking furiously until Daniel silenced her with a short command.

He turned toward Jennifer, his expression alert and wary as she clutched tightly at his arm. "Daniel, what—"

At the sound of another cry, both couples took off running, Jennifer guiding Daniel on one side as the retriever herded him on the other.

Ahead of them, the other couple stopped at the entrance to the alley for only an instant before breaking into a run again. His topcoat flapping in the wind as he raced down the alley, the man shouted as he ran. "You—what are you doing? Get away from her!"

Her heart pounding, Jennifer stumbled, catching the toe of her shoe on a loose piece of old paving brick. Pitching forward, she groped at Daniel to steady herself but didn't stop.

With terrible dread, she saw a figure near the other end of the alley. The only light was a dim ribbon filtering down from the clear night sky between the buildings, but even in the darkness she could see it was a woman. A woman on her knees, cringing as if badly frightened or injured, struggling to

25

get to her feet while clawing wildly at the side of the bank building.

"*Whitney!* Oh, no! Daniel—it's Whitney!"

Fighting for breath, her chest on fire, Jennifer surged ahead. Horrified, she saw movement in the shadows at Whitney's side. As she stared, wide-eyed, Whitney hauled herself upright, only to sink again to her knees.

Jennifer screamed, caught a glimpse of white and a flash of a grotesque face huddled close to the side of the brick building flanking the alley. The *Pierrot.*

He crouched, weaving toward Whitney as if to grab her. Abruptly he stopped, his head snapping upward when he saw the two couples almost upon him. He straightened, looking down at the woman at his feet. Then he pivoted and fled, disappearing from the alley.

By the time they reached Whitney, she had coiled herself against the side of the building, pushing her face and hands against the stone, as if trying to melt into it. Dry, heaving sobs wracked her slender body, and she was gasping harshly for breath.

Jennifer dropped down beside her, quickly wrapping Whitney in her arms as Daniel stood close-by.

Feeling the violent trembling of the thin shoulders beneath her hands, Jennifer tried to shield her with her own body, holding her as tightly as she could. She drew back just enough for Whitney to read her lips. "Whitney, what happened? Are you hurt?"

The trembling became even more violent as Whitney stared at her through blank, terrified eyes. "Whitney! Please, tell me if you're hurt!"

Finally, the stunned, panic-stricken gaze began to clear. As if she only then realized who Jennifer was, Whitney blinked, started to speak but, instead, nodded her head in a stiff, jerky gesture, saying nothing.

Feeling miserably helpless, Jennifer held her tightly,

letting her sob against her shoulder.

"Is she all right?" Daniel asked, dropping down beside them on one knee.

"I think so," Jennifer answered tremulously, looking up at the other couple standing next to them.

"We tried to see which way he went," the man said, his breathing still labored, "but he's gone. Not a sign of him." He paused, catching his breath. "I'm going to leave my wife here with you folks and go find a policeman. Be back as soon as I can."

As he hurried down the alley, his wife bent over Whitney, studying her with concern. "Is she hurt?"

Whitney was quiet now, although she continued to droop heavily against Jennifer's shoulder. "I think she's all right. Just badly frightened."

Turning to Daniel, Jennifer said in a thick, unsteady voice, "Daniel, it was the clown. The *Pierrot.*"

His face was hard as he gently stroked the retriever's head. "You saw him?"

"Oh, yes," Jennifer grated out angrily. "I saw him."

Whitney stirred, slowly easing away from Jennifer's protective arms. Glancing from Jennifer to Daniel, then to the kind-faced woman looking down at her, she touched her cheek with trembling fingers. Letting her hand drop away, she signed her words as she spoke. "How did you know... where to find me?"

Jennifer squeezed her eyes shut for an instant, then opened them. "We *didn't* know. We were about to give up when we heard you scream."

Whitney looked surprised. "You heard me?" she asked softly. "I was so frightened, I wasn't sure I actually screamed out loud."

Giving her friend another reassuring hug, Jennifer stopped when she noticed a dark bruise spreading across Whitney's cheekbone, just beneath her eye. "Whitney—your

27

face! He *hit* you!" she choked out with furious disbelief.

The look Whitney turned on her as she again lifted her hand to her cheek made Jennifer flinch. Whitney's eyes held the terror-filled, hunted look of a victim. But there was something else, some furtive, shadowed expression that inexplicably made Jennifer think of a trapped, guilty child.

Shaken, she moved to get a closer look at Whitney's face, drawing back when Whitney abruptly turned her head away.

"Jennifer?" Daniel's voice at her side reminded her that he couldn't see what was happening.

Quickly she explained. "Her face is bruised," she said in a low voice, her eyes never leaving Whitney's profile. "It looks as if it must hurt terribly."

Anger darkened his features as Daniel got to his feet. "Do you think she needs a doctor? I can call Dad."

Jennifer turned back to Whitney, touching her lightly on the arm to get her attention. "Whitney, Daniel wants to know if you want to see a doctor. We'll call Lucas if—"

Without letting her finish, Whitney quickly shook her head in protest. "No! No," she repeated in a more controlled tone of voice, "I'm . . . fine. I just want . . . to go home."

"We have to wait for the police," Daniel reminded her gently.

Whitney, watching him closely to read his lips, nodded reluctantly. Leaning on Jennifer, she pulled herself to her feet. For an instant she weaved, and Jennifer was afraid she was going to fall. But with one hand against the stone wall, she straightened, waiting as if to clear her head before turning back to Jennifer with an uncertain smile.

"I'm all right, Jennifer. Don't look so . . . worried."

"Whitney?"

At Daniel's questioning tone, Jennifer gestured to Whitney to turn toward him, so she could read his lips.

28

"Whitney, do you have any idea—any idea at all—who that clown might be? Could he possibly be someone you know?"

Whitney glanced uneasily at Jennifer. "I . . . no, I'm sure I don't know him."

Daniel pulled in a deep breath, letting it out slowly. "Do you know if he had a weapon of any kind? A gun, a knife—"

Again Whitney shook her head. "I didn't see anything like that."

Searching her expression closely, Jennifer asked, "Whitney, do you have any idea what he wanted? Why he attacked you?"

She saw something unreadable flicker in Whitney's eyes. "I think he . . . hit me because I tried to run," she said woodenly. "I think he was trying to take me . . . away, to take me . . . with him."

Chilled by Whitney's quiet, emotionless statement, Jennifer stared at her. "You think he was trying to—abduct you?"

Whitney's only answer was to nod and look away.

When Jennifer would have pressed, Daniel touched her arm. "Jennifer, she's had quite a scare, and she still has the police's questions to answer, too. Maybe you'd better give it a rest, honey."

Jennifer looked from him to Whitney. She opened her mouth, then closed it, reluctantly admitting to herself that he was probably right.

Whitney lay sleepless in the Kaine's guest room. She had tried to resist Jennifer's insistence that she stay with them, but the truth was that she had been too frightened to spend the night alone in her own house.

Turning toward the window, she stared unseeingly at the moon-dusted grove of pine trees outside. Her hand plucked

29

nervously at the bed covers. Her head spun with possibilities, all of them terrifying.

With a soft moan of frustration, she clenched her teeth, willing her mind to turn off its fast forward of tormenting memories. Her body was rigid with tension, her neck stiff, her chest tight.

She knew she didn't dare sleep tonight. If she did, the dreams would come—and the raw, agonizing fear that was an inseparable part of those nightmares. Before tonight, she had finally conquered the fear, at least the worst of it. The ugly dreams no longer tortured her; the pain no longer pursued her through sleepless hours, night after night.

It had taken months, but at last she was beginning to feel secure with her hard-won freedom from terror. Little by little she was learning to rely on the presence and the protection of the Lord.

But tonight, she knew, the memories would come again.

Please, Lord, she whispered to herself, *please help me to stop thinking about it . . . please. . . .*

It wasn't the same as the other time. Of course, it wasn't. It was just some local weirdo trying to have a little sick fun. He was probably drunk, without the vaguest idea of who she was. She had just happened along at the wrong time, that's all. He was just out to terrorize someone . . . anyone.

Restlessly, she tossed, turning over and burying her face in the pillow.

It's over . . . . It was just a freak incident, and it's over. I wasn't hurt . . . . Nothing really happened. Nothing is going to happen. It can't . . . . It can't possibly happen again . . . . Oh, Lord, you wouldn't let it happen again . . . . You wouldn't, would you?

30

3

Out of control, he hurled the clown suit across the room. The pants and tunic billowed to the floor like black and white sails ripped away from their mast.

He stood, unmoving, staring at the suit. His face felt tight and hot, as much from anger as exertion. Whirling around, he howled savagely into the empty room, punching the wall hard with his fist.

Rage thundered inside his head, thudded behind his eyes. "I should have *waited!*"

His face erupted in a frenzied spasm as his head fell back, and he again roared into the silence. "Why didn't I *wait?*"

After a moment, his fury momentarily spilled, he crossed the room and picked up the clown suit, dangling it from his fingers for an instant before tossing it onto the bed. Finally, he sank down beside it, splayed both hands on his knees and stared through the doorway into the kitchen.

Rubbing both knees mindlessly, he willed his body to wind down from the rage beating against his mind, threatening to blind him with its intensity.

"So close," he muttered, his voice dropping abruptly. "I was so close."

He began to rock back and forth on the edge of the bed, slowly and rhythmically, much like an unjustly chastised child attempting to console himself. As he rocked, his breathing slowed, the flushed splotches on his face paled, and his eyes began to clear.

Finally, he ceased rocking. He glanced down at himself

with surprise, only now aware that he was clammy and uncomfortable. The knit shirt and corduroy pants he'd been wearing beneath the clown suit were drenched with perspiration, more from the vicious hurricane in his head than the furtive escape through the streets.

He curled his mouth with distaste. Anxious to be rid of the offensive clothing, he nevertheless shivered at the thought of bathing again. The rooms were cold, and he was tired. So tired. He needed to rest, longed to crawl into bed and sleep for hours.

But in order to sleep, he had to be clean.

He rose from the bed and picked up the clown suit. This time handling it more carefully, he folded it and put it in the suitcase with its mate.

Straightening, he glanced around the room until he spied the black cap and white gloves just inside the doorway where he'd tossed them in the heat of his anger. Retrieving them, he placed them in the suitcase on top of the clown suits.

"Next time," he said softly, staring down at the open suitcase. "Next time will be different. I won't lose you again, Whitney-love."

He walked into the kitchen, catching a glimpse of himself in the shaving mirror on the table. Stopping, he postured, contorting his face into a grotesque mockery of a smiling clown. His red mouth, smeared and gaping, was a bleeding slash against the streaked white of his face. After giving himself a wide, knowing smile, he turned away, thinking.

He'd been too impatient tonight. Impatient and careless. Seeing her so close, touching her, had made him lose control, made him reckless.

He should have been patient, should have waited. His intention had been simply to watch her, perhaps tease her a little, even frighten her. But nothing else. Not yet. The nearness of her had undone him. Now she would be on guard, the very thing he didn't want.

32

He began to pull at the knuckles of first one hand, then the other, weaving the upper half of his body sideways as he kneaded his fingers.

Those people she'd been with—the blind man and the woman—where did they fit into her life? He knew about the Kaines, of course. He'd been trailing her every move for days, noting where she went, what she did. Sometimes she went to their radio station; occasionally they had lunch together. Three nights ago she had been at the Kaines' house until after eleven.

He didn't like that. He had hoped to find her entirely on her own, not getting tight with a couple of pushy do-gooders.

But he'd deal with it. Soon. And next time he wouldn't blow it. No more mistakes. From this point on, he would plan every move, every detail. He'd take it slow, be careful. Extremely careful. First he would unnerve her, put her off balance, shake her up a little. Then he'd move in and start putting on the pressure, make her crazy.

That was the part he liked best, the first act. Watching them come unglued. It gave more drama to the play, made the painful but unavoidable ending far more interesting.

With Whitney, the stage had to be set just right. With the others, it had been only repeats of the same scenarios: first punishment, followed by justice, then the final cleansing. But for Whitney, it would be different. True, the ending would be the same, but a whole new act had to be written just for her. A new and different act that would serve to balance the entire performance.

Revenge.

4

By Monday, things were back to normal, at least on the surface.

The monthly board meeting of the Friend-to-Friend Association was held that morning in the station's conference room, just as it was every month. Jennifer thought Whitney seemed understandably tense but composed throughout the meeting. Her suggestions were constructive, her comments clear and intelligent as always. Her eyes, however, were smudged with shadows, and her complexion was unhealthily pale, as if she hadn't slept well for days.

After staying Friday night with the Kaines, Whitney had spent the remainder of the weekend at her own home, in spite of Jennifer's protests. They had talked for a few minutes after church Sunday, only long enough for Whitney to report that the police had no new leads on her assailant.

It seemed to Jennifer that there was a new restraint about Whitney, or at least a subtle deepening of her usual reserve. Still, she had to agree with Daniel that any noticeable change right now was to be expected, and, hopefully, was only temporary.

The three of them had planned to have lunch together after the meeting, and Jennifer was looking forward to it. If Whitney would open up about how she was feeling, she might be able to shed some of the strain of the last few days.

Shortly after the meeting, however, Daniel stopped her in

the hallway to suggest a possible change of plans.

"Why don't you and Whitney go to lunch alone? Just the two of you."

"But I thought you wanted to come, too."

"I do, but I've got a time problem this afternoon. Besides," he said, dipping one hand into his pocket as they walked down the hall, "it might be better if you had some time alone with her. She sounds to me as if she's strung pretty tight."

Jennifer sighed. "She is. But what are you going to do about lunch?"

"I had a call early this morning from a fellow who wants to talk with me. I told him to come by about 11:30," he explained, stopping with Sunny at the door to Jennifer's office. "I'm doing Gabe's news and the 1:30 'Contact' show for the next two weeks while he and Lyss are in Huntington, so I thought if you don't mind, I'd talk with Devlin over lunch. I don't have any other free time today."

"Devlin?"

He nodded. "Michael Devlin. Says he's a photojournalist."

"What in the world is someone like that doing in Shepherd Valley?" She reached up to straighten the collar of Daniel's shirt under his crewneck sweater. "And what does he want to talk with you about?"

He shrugged, lifting his chin while she worked on his collar. "He said someone referred him to me to get some information on the town."

"You've never heard of him?"

"No, I guess he's been in town only a couple of days." He smiled as she pressed his collar into place and kissed him lightly on the cheek. "He has an accent of some sort— Australian or Irish, maybe—I'm not sure. You'll probably meet him," he said, touching the face of his Braille watch. "He should be here soon."

"Hm. Well, that's fine. We'll just go on, so I can get back

35

early in case you need me later."

"I always need you, darlin'."

"See that it stays that way."

"I think I'd like another kiss, please."

"You're a greedy man, Daniel Kaine." She raised her face for his kiss.

"Nope," he corrected her afterward. "Just a man who's in love with his wife. See you later, kid. I'm going down to the studio; Lee wants me to jock the last half of the hour with him."

She watched him, smiling at his broad back as he turned and walked down the hall with Sunny.

Jennifer bent over her desk to take a quick look at the hot clock for her afternoon show, making a minor adjustment in the last quarter hour. Katharine Chandler, Daniel's secretary, had left a couple of messages on her desk. She glanced at them, decided they could wait, then left the room to find Whitney.

At the end of the hall, she stopped just short of the doorway to the lobby. A stranger was standing at the reception desk, facing the glass-enclosed broadcasting studio. She could see only his profile, but felt it safe to assume that he was the man who had called Daniel that morning. Unfamiliar faces were rare in Shepherd Valley; this had to be Michael Devlin.

Dressed simply in a black bomber jacket, sneakers and jeans, he projected a harmless enough appearance at first glance. A closer look, however, revealed a certain... *presence* about the man that caused a shiver of unease to skate down her spine.

He was tall, lean-faced, wiry and obviously fit. His burnished complexion appeared slightly wind-whipped. His hair, thick and carelessly tousled, was a peculiar shade of rich, dark mahogany just beginning to silver at the temples. A faint hint of stubbornness hovered about strong features, while the late afternoon shadow of a beard and a mouth bracketed by two distinct lines added an air of cynicism. Oddly enough, Jennifer thought, the face stopped just short of being . . . poetic. There was a definite melancholy about him, a feeling of lost dreams and shattered hopes.

It was his eyes that banished any illusion of poetic gentleness. As if suddenly sensing her presence, he turned, focusing a green-eyed stare on her that was both brooding and sharply watchful. Jennifer got a fleeting sensation of a stealthy panther, edgy and restless with a barely controlled energy threatening to explode at any moment.

Abruptly, as if relegating her to an insignificant corner, he turned his attention back to the studio without so much as a change in expression.

Fighting another ripple of discomfort, Jennifer walked the rest of the way into the lobby. Only then, seeing the direction of his gaze, did she realize that Whitney, not the studio, was the subject of his attention. With her back turned to the reception desk, Whitney stood watching Daniel and Lee Kelsey through the studio window; she was obviously unaware of anyone else's presence in the room.

Jennifer cleared her throat, then asked, "May I help you?"

At the same time, Whitney spun around, as if she had caught a glimpse of Jennifer out of the corner of her eye.

At the sight of Whitney's face, the stranger seemed to freeze for a moment. Finally, with a stunned look, he nudged the strap of a large camera bag a little higher on his shoulder, his eyes never leaving Whitney's face.

Jennifer started to smile at him, then saw the frown he shot her as he finally managed to drag his gaze away from Whitney.

His low-set, dark brows lifted. "I'd like to see Daniel Kaine, please." A blunt, precise edge hardened what might have otherwise been a deep, even melodic voice. There was, as Daniel had indicated of his caller, an accent, a soft but distinct lilt.

"You're Mr. Devlin?"

"I am, yes."

"I'm Jennifer Kaine, Daniel's wife." With a quick glance at the studio, she saw that Daniel still had on his headset. "He's just finishing up a program; he should be off the air in a moment."

Devlin again turned his attention to Whitney, who was studying his face intently and with some bewilderment.

"This is Whitney Sharyn. Whitney is deaf, Mr. Devlin," she said quickly, feeling the need to explain.

His expression seemed to gentle. "Miss Sharyn—I'm very happy to meet you."

Whitney frowned, lifted a restraining hand to him, then touched her lips and shook her head to show Devlin she didn't understand.

"If you could speak a little slower," Jennifer suggested, "it might help. I think it's your accent. Whitney's an expert lip-reader, but it may take her a moment to get used to you."

His expression softened more as he repeated his greeting, enunciating his words more distinctly, then adding, "I'm Michael Devlin."

She gave him a shy smile and offered her hand. "I'm . . . Whitney Sharyn."

Jennifer watched in silence as Devlin pressed his fingers around Whitney's outstretched hand. The transformation in the man was amazing. Gone was the grim-faced stranger. In his place stood an unexpectedly pleasant-featured man with a boyish smile and the formidable charm of a Celtic prince.

Jennifer saw that, like most men meeting Whitney for the first time, Devlin seemed to find it difficult to tear his gaze away from her. She wasn't surprised. Her own appraisal of

Whitney's appearance, when she'd first attempted to describe her to Daniel, had included the comment that their new young director of Friend-to-Friend reminded her of an exquisitely perfect porcelain figurine.

Everything about her was delicate, feminine and achingly lovely. Whitney's beauty was sweetly elegant rather than dramatic or sensational. She had the kind of looks, Jennifer had remarked with a sigh, that undoubtedly made men want to protect her, to—cherish her.

Jennifer folded her arms and watched Michael Devlin's coat of armor drop away and melt at his feet.

She couldn't help but wonder how much longer he might have drawn out their handshake if Daniel and Sunny hadn't come out of the studio just then.

"Jennifer, did Glenn McDonald call back yet?" Holding Sunny's harness with one hand while he smoothed his dark hair with the other, he stopped just short of the reception desk.

"No, not unless he called during the meeting," she told him. "But Katharine didn't leave a note. Daniel—"

"Would you try him again? There's still a bad short in that number two suspension mike. I'm beginning to feel as though I'm sitting in the electric chair every time it's open."

"I'll call him right away. Daniel—"

"And make sure he knows it hasn't been right since he was here last week. I'm not going to pay him until he gets it fixed."

"I'll tell him. Daniel—"

"If I'm going to get electrocuted, I'd just as soon not make it a live performance." He paused. "I thought you and Whitney were going to lunch."

"We are, but—"

"Good. I thought Devlin would be here by now. I'm not going to have much time."

"Daniel, will you *listen* to me?"

He looked surprised. "What's wrong?"

"He *is* here."

"Who?"

"Mr. Devlin! He's here."

"Oh. Why didn't you tell me?" he asked mildly.

Jennifer looked at him helplessly. After a long sigh, she introduced the two men.

Dropping Sunny's harness, Daniel inclined his head and extended his hand, waiting for Devlin to take it before asking, "How can I help you?"

Jennifer watched as Devlin's eyes flicked from Daniel's face to the harnessed retriever at his side. Understanding quickly dawned in his expression.

"Mr. Kaine," he said, his tone friendly, his gaze intent as he shook Daniel's hand. "I was referred to you by a fellow over at the Commerce Office—Robinson. I'm interested in gathering some information on your community. He said you might be willing to help me."

Daniel nodded, releasing Devlin's hand. "You said on the phone that you're a journalist?"

"A photojournalist, actually. I'm doing a series of features on small Appalachian communities like your own."

"Sounds interesting. Where are you from, Mr. Devlin?"

"Michael, please," Devlin offered. "Or Dev—I answer to either. I'm from Cincinnati most recently. Belfast before that."

"Belfast—as in Ireland?"

"Northern Ireland, yes, that's right."

Jennifer noticed that while Devlin was carrying on the conversation with Daniel, his glance continued to dart to and from Whitney. She would have been amused had it not been for the disturbing undertone of secrecy he seemed to emanate. A line from a play dangled at the back of her mind . . . *A man walks out of the shadows, a dark man of secrets and night.*

She pushed the thought away at the sound of Daniel's voice. "Hal Robinson makes me sound like the local historian," he said lightly, "which I'm not. But if you'd like to have lunch, I'll try to answer whatever questions I can for you."

"Lunch? Today, do you mean?"

"Yes, in a few minutes. I have a news broadcast to do at one o'clock, so I'll need to be back by then. There's a great little restaurant nearby, just down the hill."

Devlin appeared to be caught short by Daniel's friendliness but quickly recovered. "I'd like that. I haven't eaten yet today."

"You said you've only been in town a couple of days," Daniel said. "Where are you staying?"

"I'm at a motel across town right now. The, ah, Covered Bridge—"

He broke off at Daniel's soft chuckle. "Would I be correct in assuming you'd like to find a room with a few more conveniences?"

Devlin gave a short laugh. "Actually, I'd be content with hot water." He pulled a small piece of note paper out of his jacket pocket and glanced down at it. "I've been checking the listings in the newspaper. There are two or three here that sound promising. Perhaps you could give me an idea where they are. There's one on Lee Street, and another on Greenbrier Court."

Unexpectedly, Whitney answered before Daniel could. "That's . . . my street," she said, her words coming slowly but clearly as she looked up into Devlin's face.

Michael glanced down at her. With what appeared to be a conscious effort to speak more clearly for her benefit, he asked, "Greenbrier Court? That's where you live?"

She nodded, adding, "And work. My . . . apartment is in back of the office."

Disquieted, Jennifer watched Devlin's piercing stare measure Whitney with unhurried thoroughness until Daniel's voice interrupted.

"Greenbrier's a nice street. Mostly renovated older homes and a few small business offices. It's a better area than Lee Street," he mused. "Nothing much there except some cramped one-room efficiencies."

"Then I'll try Greenbrier first," Devlin said brusquely. "I can't do with an efficiency; I need some extra space I can convert to a temporary darkroom, you see."

"You make your own prints?" asked Daniel.

Devlin nodded, then caught himself. "I do, yes."

Again hiking the strap of the camera bag a little higher on his shoulder, he turned to Whitney. "Are you a native of the area, Miss Sharyn?"

Whitney gave him a faint smile and shook her head. "I've only been here for . . . three months."

His low-set brows arched. "I don't suppose you'd be free to direct me to your neighborhood later?"

When Whitney explained that she had plans for lunch and appointments scheduled for the entire afternoon, Jennifer drew a breath of relief. For some obscure reason, Devlin made her uneasy. She rationalized her feelings with a reminder that *any* newcomer would be suspect right now, after what had happened to Whitney Friday night. Devlin was a stranger, and a somewhat intimidating stranger with his aloof curtness, his searching eyes, his apparent interest in Whitney. It was only natural to feel guarded about him.

Guarded, she admitted to herself, might not be quite strong enough for her response to Michael Devlin. Inexplicably, the man rankled her, set her on edge. For once, she was almost grateful for the marked reserve Whitney invariably displayed around men, a reserve that at times seemed to border on fearfulness. *With a man like this one,* she thought cynically, *Whitney would probably be wise to maintain her reserve at all costs.*

"Daniel, I wonder if you've a washroom close-by?" Devlin asked. "I drove out earlier this morning to get some film of the valley, and I'd like to dust myself off a bit before lunch."

"Down the hall to your right," Daniel told him, inclining his head.

After another covert glance at Whitney, Devlin left the lobby.

Once he was gone, Daniel gave an enormous stretch, saying, "How about that, ladies? Our little town may end up making a national magazine."

When Jennifer didn't answer, he dropped his arms back to his sides and asked, "What does he look like?"

She hesitated, then said evenly, "Tall, trim, young—early thirties, I suppose."

"That's vague enough."

She looked at him. "He's—" she faltered, "—difficult to describe. Not physically," she explained. "But there's something about him . . . ."

"Uh-oh," Daniel cracked with a grin, "here comes the character study."

Ignoring him, she finished. "He looks—remote."

"Remote?" Daniel repeated with a dubious lift of one dark brow.

"Remote—and perhaps a little angry," she said more firmly. Then she added, "I don't know that he's a man I'd trust."

At Daniel's puzzled expression, Jennifer shot a questioning glance at Whitney, who had been reading their lips intently.

Whitney met her look with a small, uncertain nod of agreement, her gaze going to the hallway door which Devlin

43

had just exited. Hesitantly, she added a comment of her own, her voice so soft Jennifer could scarcely make out her words.

"He has pain . . . in his eyes, though. Did you see?"

It was then that Jennifer realized with uneasy surprise that Whitney hadn't demonstrated even a hint of her usual reserve with Michael Devlin.

5

"You did *what?*"

Jennifer leaned forward, pressing the palms of both hands onto the top of Daniel's desk as she stared at him incredulously. The late afternoon sun spilled through the open drapes of the window behind him, framing his head and shoulders in an intense golden aura, making the bronze of his cheeks even deeper, the blue of his eyes even clearer.

As if surprised by her reaction, he knit his brows together in a small frown. "I invited him to the house for pizza Wednesday night," he repeated mildly.

Had she not been so exasperated with the man, Jennifer might have allowed herself a moment to study her husband with affection. His face, now sculpted in autumn amber, posed an intriguing blend of strength and gentleness, wisdom and humor, as well as a maturity that had been finely carved from a faith long-tested and found true. Perturbed as she was with him, however, she permitted herself only the briefest response to his appeal.

"Why on earth would you do that, Daniel?" she exclaimed, leaning even farther over his desk. "You just met him this morning. Michael Devlin is a stranger to us."

With infuriating calm, he steepled his fingers together to support his chin. "I invited him for pizza, Jennifer; I didn't ask him to move in."

"Still—"

"He's new in town," he reminded her patiently, much in the same tone of voice she'd heard him use with Jason when

45

he was trying to explain a difficult concept. "He doesn't know anyone except us, and I thought it would be a nice gesture."

"Didn't you remember that we've already asked Whitney to come home with us after prayer meeting?"

"I remembered," he said casually. "Why? Do you think she'll mind?"

Would she mind? Jennifer wasn't sure. She was still puzzled by the noticeable lack of reserve Whitney had exhibited toward Devlin that morning. As guarded as she normally appeared to be around most men, at least those she didn't know, why hadn't she shown more wariness with the enigmatic photographer?

"What if *I* mind?"

Movement from Sunny, lying next to Daniel's chair, caught her attention. The retriever, her head raised, her ears pricked, was regarding Jennifer with troubled brown eyes. When the dog whimpered softly, Jennifer felt a pinch of guilt; her tone must have been much sharper than she'd intended.

Daniel's expression cleared, and he smiled a little. "Maybe you'd feel better about him if I told you something I learned while we were at lunch."

Immediately interested, Jennifer sank down in the chair across from his desk. "I'm listening."

Locking his hands comfortably behind his head, Daniel leaned back in the worn, oversized leather chair that had served his grandfather, the station's founder, for a number of years before Daniel had inherited both the chair and the station.

"Devlin's an ex-cop," he said easily, hoisting one impressively large foot onto the top of his desk.

"A *policeman?*" Jennifer stared at him blankly. Of everything she might have expected to hear about the dark-haired Irishman, nothing like this would have occurred to her.

Daniel nodded. "A *constable,* I believe he called it. In Belfast."

"Did he say why he left?"

He gave a nonchalant shrug. "Not really. He mentioned something about all the violence."

"And of course you didn't try to learn anything more than what he volunteered?"

A ghost of a smile began to tease the corners of his mouth. "Of course, I didn't."

Jennifer squirmed a little at the thought that her reaction to this information bordered on *resentment,* almost as if she didn't want to hear any redeeming facts about Devlin. Pushing the feeling aside, she commented, "He's made a rather drastic change in career direction, hasn't he? From an Irish policeman to a freelance photojournalist, or whatever he says he is."

Shaking his head, he laughed softly. "You never quit, do you?"

"Well, *I* would have asked more questions than I'm sure *you* did," she said defensively.

"Oh, I don't doubt that for a minute, darlin'."

"So all you really know about this man is that he's someone who *says* he used to be a policeman, who now goes around taking pictures and writing stories."

Jennifer had seen that long-suffering, groping-for-patience smile at various times in their relationship and was wholly undaunted by it. "*Well?*" she pressed.

A flash of mischief darted across his face. "At this point, Devlin's dossier includes only significant data: He uses a good aftershave; he doesn't smoke; and he doesn't seem to crack his knuckles or grind his teeth, at least not audibly."

She made a sound of disgust.

Sighing deeply, Daniel added, "There's not much else, Jennifer. He's apparently doing some kind of a special series on Appalachian settlements. Said he'd be in the area a few weeks, taking pictures, interviewing people, sniffing out some human interest stories—that sort of thing." With a light shrug, he added, "That's about it. That, and the fact that he's coming to our house for pizza Wednesday night."

She leaned forward on the chair. "Since he's going to eat with us, I assume he's going to church with us, too?"

Daniel dropped his hands from behind his head and rested them on the chair arms, lowering his foot from the desk back to the floor. "He is," he answered somewhat hesitantly, "but to be honest, I got the feeling he agreed to go only when he found out Whitney would be there."

"That wouldn't surprise me at all," she snapped, "considering the fact that he couldn't tear his eyes away from her in the lobby this morning!" She broke off, then muttered caustically, "I wonder if he's even a Christian."

His answer wasn't what she expected. "Yes, he is. The conversation about Wednesday night's prayer meeting gave me a chance to ask him," he explained. "He said he was raised in a Christian home and came to know the Lord around age nine. But I got the distinct impression that he didn't want to talk about it. He changed the subject pretty fast once he'd answered my question."

Neither of them spoke for a long moment. Finally Daniel tipped his head and patted the arm of his chair. "Come here," he said quietly.

She got up and walked around the desk, stooping to scratch Sunny's ears for a moment before perching on the arm of the chair. "Daniel, don't be cross with me. I can't help it if I don't trust this man. And I can't help worrying about Whitney. You know she's special to me."

"I understand that, honey," he said, covering her hand with his. "But I've never known you to be this suspicious about anyone before. What's got you so uptight about Michael Devlin?"

His question made her stop to think. After a moment, she

said, "I suppose I'm frightened. For Whitney," she explained.

At last giving vent to the thought that had been troubling her ever since the Irish journalist had walked into the station that morning, she said, "I don't think I could trust anyone we don't know right now, Daniel. Hasn't it occurred to you that Devlin could be the man who attacked Whitney?"

His expression grew more serious. Squeezing her hand, he admitted, "Sure, I've thought of it. But I think we've got to realize that *anyone* could have been wearing that clown suit the other night. There's no reason to assume it was someone we don't know."

"Did you mention the attack on Whitney to Devlin?" she asked abruptly.

He nodded. "We talked about it."

"How did he react?"

He thought for a moment. "He sounded genuinely shocked, maybe even angry. But he's not a man who displays his feelings very openly, you know. He's more—" He stopped, seeming to fumble for the word he wanted.

"Aloof," she finished for him. "*Cold.*"

He shook his head. "No, I don't think so," he said firmly. Drumming the fingers of his free hand on the other chair arm, he changed the subject. "Jennifer, there's something else about Friday night. You believe the attack on Whitney was preplanned, that it was personal, don't you?"

With a questioning frown, she studied his face. "Don't *you?*"

He shrugged. "Not necessarily. Whitney could have simply been in the wrong place at the wrong time. The creep who jumped her may not even have known her name. He might have just been looking for a woman to terrorize—*any* woman, not Whitney in particular."

Jennifer sorted through his remarks one at a time, gradually conceding the possibility that he might be right. If it was a random assault, the danger was over.

49

It jolted her to realize how much she hoped he *was* right. The idea of Whitney being singled out for some horrible, incomprehensible reason was far more terrifying than an unpremeditated attack.

She looked at him. "We've spent a lot of time discussing *my* feelings about Michael Devlin. What about *yours?* You're the one who had lunch with him. How do *you* feel about him?"

Still holding her hand, he pressed his lips into a thoughtful line and said carefully, "You don't get to know much about a person in an hour. But at this point, I'd have to say that I found myself drawn to the man."

"But, Daniel, you don't *know* him!" she interrupted impulsively.

He lifted one dark brow and replied in a quiet, even voice. "Neither do you, Jennifer, but it seems to me that you've made up your mind *not* to like him."

Wincing at the justified rebuke, Jennifer pulled in a deep breath, saying nothing.

Daniel went on. "You asked me how I feel about Devlin. First, I believe he fancies himself to be a rather hard man, but I imagine that's an occupational hazard with anyone who's ever been involved in law enforcement. I get a sense of a man who's keenly intelligent, perhaps smart enough to keep you from finding out just how sensitive he really is. He's direct, professional, and I would guess extremely capable." He paused, then added, "A little cynical, I think. And a loner."

He shifted slightly in his chair. "To be honest, I think I'd like to get to know him better."

"Well, I still don't think it's such a great idea," she said grudgingly, "having him come to the house so soon— especially when you think he may only be interested in Whitney."

He lifted both hands in a palms up gesture of hopeless-ness. "And I said *Devlin* is hard?" Laughing, he pulled her onto his lap.

"Daniel, someone might come in!"

Ignoring her, he bundled her snugly in the circle of his arms. "In case you've forgotten, darlin', we're married. That makes it perfectly all right for you to sit on my lap."

"Katharine—"

"—is already gone for the day." He kissed her lightly, tightening his embrace even more.

"Mm." Enjoying the closeness and the wonderfully secure fortress of his powerful arms, Jennifer stroked her cheek against the soft ivory fleece of his shirt. Her weak protest was more a purr. "Still, someone could walk in."

"No one's here but us." He kissed her again.

Jennifer allowed herself one more long moment of closeness before drawing back and prodding his chest with a stern finger. "Daniel, I want you to promise me that you'll be careful. About Devlin. You won't—trust him too much too quickly, will you? Just in case?"

Laughing, he tapped her gently on the end of her nose. "My sweet Jennifer, you are an absolutely relentless mother hen. You can't resist sad-eyed strays or lost souls, can you?"

"Well, I'm afraid I can't always be as effective as I'd like to be with lost souls," she admitted with a sigh, "but I guess I *am* a pushover for sad-eyed strays."

Clasping both of her shoulders, he pushed her gently from his lap as he got to his feet. Smiling, he circled her waist with his hands. "Is that why you married me?"

Her mood suddenly turning playful, she countered, "Of course not. I married you because you're an absolutely devastating man."

"Yeah?" His grin was pleased, if a little foolish, as he pulled her slightly closer. "Devastating, huh?"

"Oh, yes. Definitely devastating."

51

Seemingly satisfied with her assurance, he nodded. "Was that the only reason?"

"Well, no. Actually, there was one other thing."

Dropping his hands away from her waist, he crossed his arms over his chest, lifted his chin and prompted, "And what, exactly, was that 'one other thing'?"

"Job security," she said matter-of-factly, flicking a piece of red sweater fuzz—her own—from his shoulder as she touched a light kiss to his bearded cheek. "A girl has to be practical, you know."

"Oh, absolutely," he agreed, tossing an arm around her shoulder as they started out of the office. "It's a jungle out there."

6

"Why don't you just stay here tonight?" Jennifer urged, following Whitney outside with obvious reluctance. "It's late, and I'd feel so much better—"

"If I were under your watchful eye," Whitney finished for her with an affectionate grin, moving to embrace her. "Will you stop worrying about me? I'm fine."

Jennifer clung to her for a moment more, then held her at arm's length to study her face. "How do you think the evening went?"

"I think it went very well," Whitney assured her, meaning it. "You didn't insult . . . Michael Devlin more than once. All of us are going away five pounds heavier, thanks to Daniel's awesome pizza. And Jason got to stay up an hour . . . past his bedtime. If that's not a successful evening, what is?"

Jennifer wrinkled her nose at her. "Jason spent most of his extra hour shadowing Devlin. He certainly seemed to take a liking to him, did you notice?"

Nodding, Whitney agreed. "I'd say it was mutual, considering the way he turned over that expensive looking camera outfit to Jason so he could take pictures of Sunny."

"I have to admit he turned out to be a lot more personable than I expected," Jennifer answered with a sigh. "You could almost say he was good company, if you wanted to be generous."

Whitney giggled softly. "You're a hard woman, Jennifer Kaine."

Jennifer cocked her head to one side and subjected

Whitney to a thorough, narrow-eyed examination. "So what do *you* think of Devlin?"

"I think," Whitney said still smiling, "that the poor man had better watch his back around you. That's what I think."

"That does *not* an answer make, my crafty friend."

"It's too late for great thoughts, Jennifer. I'm going home."

The brown eyes narrowed even more. "Are you being evasive?"

"With you?" Whitney laughed. "I wouldn't waste my time even trying." Giving her a friendly pat on the shoulder, she said, "I *do* have to go, Jennifer. Thanks again for everything."

Jennifer managed one more parting shot before Whitney could step off the porch. "He's interested in you, you know. He hardly took his eyes off you all evening."

Flustered, Whitney tried to ignore the unexpected thud of her heart at Jennifer's statement. Forcing another smile, she said a hasty goodnight and turned to go before Jennifer could stop her.

As she backed out of the driveway and started down the hill, she realized that Jennifer's comment about Devlin had shaken her more than she cared to admit. Especially in light of her conflicting feelings toward him.

It was rare—extremely rare—for her to slip into a comfortable conversation with a man she scarcely knew. Yet tonight she'd been able to do just that with Michael Devlin. Considering her usual apprehension around strange men, she found herself at a loss to account for her response to the Irish journalist.

As she approached the bottom of the hill, she flipped on the heater's fan switch, shivering at the noisy blast of cold air that belched out at her. She stopped, checked the intersection, then turned onto Keystone Drive. Tapping her fingers rhythmically on the steering wheel, she let her thoughts return to Devlin.

He is a former policeman, she reminded herself. *Doesn't that fact give his credibility an automatic boost?*

Probably. Odd, how much easier she found it to imagine the restless, wary-eyed Devlin as a policeman rather than a nomadic freelance photographer. His somewhat hard, cynical appearance, his almost abrasive directness, and the aura of physical power emanating from him all worked together to create a distinct mantle of authority. Whitney thought he must have made a formidable opponent for any criminal.

He had been surprisingly gentle with *her,* though, she mused, recalling his obvious attempts throughout the evening to put her at ease. There had been only one bad moment, when he had unknowingly moved from an innocent conversation about her deafness into a part of her life Whitney refused to discuss with anyone, even Jennifer.

Daniel had gone to hear Jason's bedtime prayers, while Jennifer made fresh coffee. Whitney was sitting on the couch, staring at a thick log blazing in the fireplace when Devlin walked over to the hearth.

Turning his back to the fire, he dipped his hands into his pockets and stood, openly studying her.

"Daniel tells me you've been deaf since you were a child," he said bluntly. "How is it that you can speak so clearly?"

"I didn't lose my hearing until I was five," she answered, starting to sign her words as she spoke, then stopping. "By that time, you've stored quite a lot of audible speech memory."

He nodded, watching her intently. "Do you mind talking about it?"

She shook her head. "No. What I mind is for people to deliberately *avoid* talking about it." She was comfortable with his directness, in fact appreciated it. People usually found it difficult to even acknowledge her handicap, much

55

less question her about it.

"What caused it?" he asked. "Illness?"

"Meningitis," she replied, glancing into the fire for a moment before returning her attention to him. "A particularly nasty case of it."

He shifted his weight from one foot to the other, frowning. "You can't hear anything at all?"

"No. My residual hearing wasn't enough to amplify."

"With a hearing aid, you mean?"

"That's right. If there's even a small degree of residual hearing, it can often be increased with the use of a hearing aid. That wasn't a possibility in my case."

He looked down at the hearth, then back at her face. "I'm amazed at your lip-reading ability, the way you keep up with the conversation going on around you."

Whitney set her coffee cup down on the table beside the couch. "I taught a class of deaf teenagers for three years," she told him, smiling at the memory. "That experience went a long way in honing my lip-reading to a state-of-the-art skill."

The deep lines bracketing both sides of his mouth creased to a quick smile. "Yes, I can see how it would."

He came to sit down on the couch, an arm's length from her. When he turned to her, his look was contemplative and not altogether impersonal.

"Where did you teach, Whitney?" he asked. "Here, in Shepherd Valley?"

She hesitated. "No. In—in . . . Louisville, Kentucky." She flinched at the halting stammer that suddenly gripped her. "Th-that's where I'm from."

"Really?" His brow lifted. "We weren't all that far away from each other, then."

She gave him a questioning look, then remembered. "That's right," she said quickly, hoping to change the subject. "You mentioned living in Cincinnati. Was that right after you left Belfast?"

56

He nodded distractedly, his eyes still fastened on her face. Clearly, he intended to steer the conversation back to her. "So you relocated because of your new position?"

Whitney's throat tightened. Not trusting her voice, she gave a brief nod.

"You must have had quite a period of adjustment."

She looked at him sharply. "What?"

His gaze didn't waver. "The change in lifestyles," he qualified. "Moving from a metropolitan area into such a rural setting. Wasn't that difficult for you?"

She relaxed a little. "Oh. No, not really. I like it here . . . very much."

"Yes, it's a lovely place," he answered vaguely, watching her. After a moment, he draped his arm along the back of the couch and said, "I'm hoping you'll allow me to spend some time with you."

She shot him a startled look, and his eyes narrowed as if to measure her reaction. "Daniel's told me quite a lot about the Association you work for," he explained quickly. "I'm intrigued by the concept. It's rather a novel idea, isn't it—the handicapped helping the handicapped?"

Whitney let out a relieved breath. "Yes, I suppose it is, although there are a number of similar organizations springing up throughout the country." Choosing her words carefully, she went on. "You'd be welcome to visit the office, of course. But I'm afraid you'd be . . . disappointed. The actual work is done almost entirely on a one-to-one basis, among the members. I'm simply a coordinator."

"Still, I'd be interested in looking into it," he insisted with a disarming smile. "Perhaps I can get you a bit of free publicity in one of the nationals while I'm about it."

"Publicity? No," she said quickly. "I don't think we'd be interested in that."

He looked surprised. "I should think an organization like yours would welcome the exposure—to help generate additional donations."

"We don't depend on publicity for funding, Mr. Devlin—"

"*Michael,*" he reminded her firmly, his eyes probing her gaze. "I'd still like to spend a day with you at your office, if it wouldn't be too much bother."

To Whitney's enormous relief, Daniel returned just then, making it unnecessary for her to answer.

The rest of the evening had been pleasant enough, but in spite of Devlin's irreproachable manners, he unnerved her. In some inexplicable way, his presence triggered an edginess in her that, although less oppressive than the distrust she often felt toward other men, made her feel strangely awkward and unsure of herself.

It was his eyes, she realized as she slowed for the caution light at Midmount and Keystone. A deep, brilliant green, they seemed to deflect all attention from his lean face, drawing her, capturing her with a searching, relentless intensity that was like being pulled into some sort of magnetic field. More than once tonight she had been jolted by an unpleasant, irrational sensation that this man knew her, knew everything about her.

In spite of its few tense moments, however, the evening seemed to have served as a turning point in helping her to regain a measure of peace and calm for the first time in days. It was almost as if tonight had begun a healing process, a cleansing from the horror and foreboding she'd been living with ever since Friday night's attack.

Until tonight, she had begun to slide all too easily into her previous trap of self-isolation, allowing fear to force her into a panicky solitude that would quickly become routine, if she allowed it. Tonight had acted as a restraint, a wedge to block the door that had been rapidly closing on her hard-won independence.

Thank you, Lord, for intervening . . . for reminding me that I can't go back to the old way. I promised you that I would never again allow myself to be buried alive by fear.

Help me to keep that promise, Lord.

As terrifying as Friday night had been, it was only an obscene coincidence, nothing more. It had nothing to do with the other time. Friday night she had simply been a victim, not a . . . target, like before. She mustn't let the horror of a moment make her run away from life a second time.

Coming to the four way stop at Jackson and Keystone, she braked, then turned left onto Jackson Drive. Ever mindful of her inability to hear sirens or other traffic noise, she glanced in the rearview and side mirrors to check her surroundings, noting with surprise a solitary pair of headlights not too far behind. As she watched, the double beams of light moved up until they were within a car's length behind her.

She kept one eye on the mirror as she drove. When the headlights continued to follow her all the way up Jackson Drive, Whitney felt the first stirring of unease. The darkness was thick, and it was late enough that there was no traffic and few house lights to be seen.

As she approached the next intersection, she tapped the brake to stop, looked both ways, then turned right onto Greenbrier, swallowing against the dryness in her mouth when she saw that the headlights in the rearview mirror were still with her.

Halfway up the block, however, she saw the other vehicle slow, then turn into a narrow alley that dissected Greenbrier on the left. With a shaky breath, she let her shoulders sag with relief as she relaxed against the back of the seat. Running an unsteady hand through her hair, she eased her foot away from the gas pedal to slow her speed. She would soon be home.

Greenbrier Court was an old money street with a turn-of-the-century elegance. Whitney never drove down it without feeling an odd sense of satisfaction, as if she had a vested interest in the neighborhood. Twin rows of rambling, late Victorian two-stories lined the paved brick street with unpretentious dignity. Brick, white frame, or brownstone, without exception all the houses fronted the street with heavy double doors and precisely draped windows. Their nobility had been retained, even in the structures that had been converted to apartments or professional offices.

As she pulled up in front of the enormous white frame Gothic that housed the offices of Friend-to-Friend and her apartment, Whitney again glanced in the rearview mirror. Seeing nothing, she turned the engine off and pulled her keys from the ignition, snapping the top two buttons of her jacket-vest before getting out of the car.

The house sat on an elevated bank, removed several feet from the street. Whitney ran up the cracked cement steps, opened the wrought iron gate, then hurried down the walk that bordered the left side of the house. A dim light glowed from the side porch at the rear, the entrance to her apartment.

She had her key ready. Unlocking the door with one hand, she fumbled for the wall switch just inside the landing with the other. Flipping on the light as she entered, she turned to close the door behind her.

Light from a frosted glass globe overhead illuminated the narrow landing, a tired little cubicle with worn carpet and dusty rose wallpaper. Quickly, she secured the push-button lock on the knob, then slipped the latch bolt and secuity chain in place.

She stood just inside the door for a moment, her fingers resting lightly on its painted white surface. Surprised by the intensity of fear she felt at the thought of the waiting dark apartment, she pulled in a deep, steadying breath, turned, and leaned back against the door for another moment.

Finally, she shrugged out of her jacket and tossed it onto the scarred walnut coat tree in the landing. Her glance went to one of her few extravagances, a small legless desk with a high back full of pigeonholes that was securely fastened to the wall beside the coat rack. Then she turned to face the living room, dark beyond its open French doors.

For a moment she hesitated. Then, taking one more deep breath, she walked into the thickly shadowed room.

There was no overhead light, so she went to the table beside the couch and fumbled for the switch on the handpainted Victorian lamp.

Standing perfectly still, she scanned the unabashedly feminine room. Whitney had sacrificed a certain amount of style for comfort. The two plump floral chairs by the fireplace were of no particular period, but she had bought them years before because the soft mauve and cream print appealed to her. The bookshelves behind the chairs held a wide variety of titles, including a few worn volumes of her favorite children's stories. She'd left the heavy cream-toned drapes at the four-over-four window, exchanging the fussy lace undercurtains for pale ivory sheers.

Still edgy, she walked into the breakfast nook that joined the living room and kitchen. Turning on the overhead light, she let her gaze sweep the room as she removed the morning newspaper from the table. Though little more than an oversized pantry, this was her favorite room in the house. It was the place she invariably came to when she wanted to sketch or write letters or simply sit by the large bay window and think.

With growing confidence, she walked into the kitchen, folding the paper and dropping it onto a stack of others beside the door. It was an enormous room, far too spacious for her needs, but typical of the period. Modernization had been limited to fresh lemon and white paint, a free-standing stove and refrigerator, both white, and a good vinyl floor that was easy to clean.

Leaving the kitchen, she crossed the narrow hall to the

bath, giving it only a cursory check, except for a sheepish look behind the pink and white polka-dotted shower curtain.

Entering her bedroom, she crept carefully across the hardwood floor until she reached the edge of the hooked rug near the bed. The faint smell of fabric softener hovered about the room from the fresh linen she'd just put on that morning.

Her hand knocked against the glass bottom of the bedside lamp as she groped for the switch. She was staring directly at the bed when she turned on the light, but at first she didn't see the grotesque sight sprawled in the middle of the comforter. Even when reality forced its way into her mind, she stood staring in blank disbelief for a full minute before uttering a choked, terror-stricken cry.

The doll was long, at least two feet, with a delicately slender body. The costume was monstrously correct: white pants, black and white tunic, complete with a fussy white ruff and a small black skullcap. The worst part was the face. Painted in clown white, its eyes were slashed with black; its mouth was a blood-red streak. A *Pierrot* doll.

It lay flat on its back, staring up at her with a hideously evil smile. In its left hand lay one long dead rose. The other hand held a knife, small but dreadfully authentic.

Bewilderment turned to terror. The room was freezing, her chest on fire, her throat too numb to scream. She went rigid, then began to shake so violently she thought her heart would explode. Still she couldn't force her eyes away from the doll.

The blinking light of her signaling system abruptly cracked her silent horror. When the flashing lamp alerted her that her TDD phone was ringing, she screamed, then whirled around. Her eyes wild with fear, she looked from the lamp to the phone, then back to the bed.

Panicky, unable to tear her gaze away from the doll, she

62

backed up to the night table, fumbling for the phone. Suddenly the lamp stopped flashing. She had waited too long.

Then she saw the note lying beneath the doll's right hand.

With as much loathing as if she were picking up a copperhead, she slipped the note out from under the cold porcelain hand, biting her lip to ward off hysteria.

She straightened and read the message through a blurred screen of terror . . . .

"You weren't here when I came for you, Whitney-love. But that's all right. I'm leaving a gift for you, something to keep you company until I come back. Next time, I'll make sure you're here before I come in. Wait for me, Whitney. I'll be back."

Her legs started to buckle beneath her, and she grabbed at the night table to keep from falling. *It can't be . . . .*

Beneath the panic that roared across the pathway of her mind, a violent churning of outrage began to beat against her consciousness.

With glazed eyes, she stood staring at the paper in her hand. Her throat filled with hot bile, and she began to shake her head furiously back and forth in denial.

No . . . it's not him . . . it can't be him . . . no . . . oh, no, Lord, no . . . .

A sound, half-whimper, half-gag, ripped from her throat as a spasm of nausea gripped her. She shuddered, letting the note slip from her trembling hand and drift slowly to the floor. She started backing up toward the open doorway. Like a broken marionette, her legs jerked stiffly, woodenly, as she retreated.

Suddenly she stopped, turning toward the door in confusion.

Should she leave the room? What if he were still in the apartment?

She froze. No. He couldn't be inside. She had gone through the entire apartment as soon as she came in. Besides, what good would it do to lock herself inside the bedroom? She couldn't hear; she had no way of knowing what was going on in the rest of the house. He could be anywhere . . . in the front office . . . upstairs.

She glanced up at the ceiling. All those vacant rooms on the second floor . . . nothing up there except supplies and old files. He could be up there . . . hiding . . . waiting.

Seized by another thought, she stood suspended between the unknown beyond the open door and the protective cocoon of her bedroom. *How did he get inside the house?*

The doors were locked when she left, still locked when she came home.

The office. She hadn't checked the office door. It could be standing wide open for all she knew. And the connecting door between the office and her apartment was a joke. The ancient, flimsy lock wouldn't keep out a stray cat.

She covered her mouth with the back of her hand, muffling a broken sob against the damp cold of her skin.

Call Jennifer.

For an instant she considered it. It would only take a few moments for them to get across town.

No! Remember what happened to the last person who tried to help you?

She moaned. Hunching her shoulders forward, she crossed her arms tightly over her chest and clawed at her own shoulders.

If it was—him, if he was back, she had to keep Jennifer and Daniel from finding out. It would be like before. Anyone who tried to help her would be in danger . . . she couldn't do that, *wouldn't* do that to them.

What, then? She had to do *something* . . . she couldn't simply wait until he came for her.

Stop it! It's *not* him! It can't be him. They wouldn't have let him out. He's insane . . . dangerous. It's someone else, a sick joke . . . not him . . . it can't be him.

She'd call the police.

She whirled toward the phone. No. The police would come, they'd ask her questions. They'd grill her, dig at her past, find out about before. Everyone would know. Jennifer and Daniel would know. They'd try to help. The police wouldn't leave it alone, not after Friday night's attack.

Friday night.

It *had* been him. Not someone else. Not a horrible coincidence. Not a monstrous joke.

Cory.

Dear Lord, no. Please, no . . . .

The lamp began to flash again, faster . . . faster.

She cried out, then whirled around to stare at the blinking light. For a long moment, she watched. It stopped, then started flashing again.

She looked from the lamp to the doll. Evil smiled back at her.

He was in the house. She had to get out.

Whitney bolted from the room, ran down the narrow hall toward the front of the apartment.

At the back of her mind, she knew she should find a place to hide and stay there, stay quiet.

No. He'd find her. There was no place to hide. There had *never* been any place to hide.

She sprinted through the living room, to the landing. Fumbled with the chain, slid the bolt, twisted the knob.

Only when she threw open the door and saw him standing there, a dark and hulking silhouette looming in the doorway, did she realize that in the frenzy of her irrational fear, she'd made a terrible mistake.

The second sequence of flashing lights, rapid and in triple-time, wasn't the telephone alert. It was the signal system for the doorbell.

7

She tried to squeeze past him, but he spread his arms to stop her. When she tried to duck under one, he caught her by the waist, trapping her.

Whitney exploded, slapping, punching, sobbing wildly as she struck at him.

He let go of her waist, grabbed both wrists with one hand, and held her. Taking a step inside the door, he forced her backward, into the light. The collar of his dark jacket was drawn up high around his neck. His face was a granite mask, set in a frown that could have issued from either anger or surprise.

Devlin!

He pushed her back another step, his eyes burning into hers. "Whitney—what's wrong?"

She tried to say his name, but she was paralyzed. Unable to catch a breath, she felt her head reel and the room begin to spin.

"Whitney! What is it? What's happened?"

She stared at him. *Devlin, not Cory . . . .*

He stared back at her. His mouth was grim, his eyes on fire. Still holding her captive by the wrists, he glanced over his shoulder. Kicking one leg out behind him, he shut the door.

Slowly, he released her wrists, studying her relentlessly as he brought both hands up to grasp her firmly by the shoulders.

Whitney shuddered, shrinking beneath his touch.

His eyes narrowed. "What's frightened you so? Whitney—"

66

Suddenly seized by a violent trembling, she looked away from him. Nausea clutched her throat, and she swallowed down the taste of her own fear.

Devlin dropped one hand away from her shoulder, at the same time tightening his grasp on the other. Gently, he tipped her chin with his finger, making her face him.

"What's going on? Are you hurt?" His eyes darted from Whitney's face to scan their surroundings.

She opened her mouth, tried to speak, but the sound froze in her throat.

Frowning, he wrapped an arm around her shoulder and began to move her into the living room, half-carrying her. With a gentle but firm touch, he pushed her down onto the couch, then sat down beside her.

Bracing one arm on the back of the couch, he leaned toward her.

Instinctively, Whitney flinched and drew back.

His frown deepened, but he made no attempt to touch her. Waiting until she again met his gaze, he said, "Tell me."

She couldn't stop shaking. The temperature in the room seemed to be plummeting by the second.

Devlin glanced around, then rose from the couch and crossed to one of the fireside chairs. Taking a folded afghan from the back of the chair, he returned, bent over her, and gently draped the afghan around her shoulders. Again, he sat down next to her.

Grateful for the warmth, Whitney clasped the afghan to her throat with one hand.

"Better?" he asked, his gaze going over her face.

After an instant, she nodded, wrapping the afghan even more snugly around her.

He waited, the hand on his knee clenching and unclenching as he watched her.

Finally, he shifted, dipping his head slightly to get her attention. "Tell me what happened, Whitney."

Huddled under the afghan, she tensed, looked away. She couldn't possibly tell him. She didn't even know him.

Forcing her voice, keeping her eyes cast down, she finally managed to speak. "Please . . . I . . . I can't."

He didn't answer. Whitney could feel his eyes on her.

She glanced up. Surprised, she saw that his expression appeared to be deeply concerned, even troubled.

"Whitney—" he stopped, then went on. "Are you sure that you can't tell me?"

Slowly, she lifted her gaze from his lips to meet his eyes.

His look was steady—and unexpectedly gentle.

It would be foolish to tell him. Even more foolish to trust him. Besides, what could he do?

"Whitney—I might be able to help, if you'd only trust me."

No one could help. She was living a nightmare from which she'd never awaken. It was going to go on forever.

"Tell me what's wrong," he prompted again.

"W-why . . . why are you here?" she asked him abruptly. "When you left Jennifer's, you said you were going back to your apartment, to develop some film."

As if he weren't sure how to answer her, he looked away for an instant, then returned his searching gaze to her face. "I decided to drive around for a bit," he told her. "At night, especially, I like to just—drive around and see what's going on."

At her dubious look, he attempted a smile and added, "I *was* on my way home. I told you I took rooms just down the street—"

She nodded, and he went on. "I was driving past your house and saw the lights flashing in back. I thought something might be wrong, so I stopped."

"How long . . . were you here, before I answered the door?" Reading his lips, she watched his expression carefully.

68

"Not long, actually," he replied. "A few moments, no more. I assumed you were at home—I saw your car in front—so I was a little worried when you didn't come to the door right away. Then I remembered you couldn't hear the bell. I decided to leave and call the Kaines to let them know about the lights I'd seen, have them check on you. I was about to go when you came to the door."

"Did you—" She stopped, then changed her question. "How many times did you ring the bell?"

He hesitated, then replied, "Twice, I believe. But if you can't hear the bell, how did you know—"

"I have a signaling system," she interrupted. The violent trembling had finally stopped, and she was beginning to think a little more clearly. "It's hooked up so that certain lights flash . . . in different sequence, depending on whether it's . . . the doorbell or the telephone that's ringing."

"I see." He seemed to consider what she'd said for an instant, then asked, "The light that was blinking earlier, when I drove by—that was your telephone?"

She nodded. That would have been when she was in the bedroom . . . with the doll.

Watching her, he said, "When you opened the door, you were terrified. You still haven't told me why."

Whitney felt an urgency in his gaze, an intensity that somehow made her feel both threatened and protected at the same time. Surprising herself, she told him.

"Someone . . . " she faltered, swallowed, then tried again. "Someone was . . . here . . . in the house, while I was gone tonight."

It was as if she had suddenly yanked a string attached to him. His shoulder jerked, his chin lifted, and his eyes went from fire to ice. "What do you mean? How do you know?"

For the first time since she'd walked into the bedroom and confronted the horrifying sight on her bed, Whitney felt her fear give way to a swell of anger. "He left a . . . calling card," she said bitterly.

"Where?" His eyes swept the room, then returned to her.

"It's . . . in my bedroom," she said, starting to shrug out from under the afghan.

He leaped to his feet, put a restraining hand on her shoulder. "Stay here. He could still be in the house."

"No," she told him, standing and tossing the afghan onto the couch. "I checked every room as soon as I came home, like I always . . . " She stopped, not wanting him to know she lived much of her life on guard.

He looked at her. "Stay here," he said again, already moving. "Which way is your room?"

Pointing to the doorway that led into the breakfast room, she said, "Through there. Across the hall from the kitchen."

He returned empty-handed after only a few moments. Stopping in the doorway between the breakfast nook and the living room, he said, "Give me a bag of some sort, would you? A plastic sack will do."

Whitney looked at him blankly.

"For the doll. I want to slip it and the note into something so I don't lose any fingerprints that might be on them."

He followed her to the kitchen, where she gave him a plastic trash bag.

"Wait here," he said shortly as he turned to leave the room. "There's no need for you to see it again."

Whitney sank down weakly on one of the chairs at the kitchen table and waited.

When he came back, he was carrying the sack by the knot he'd tied in the top of it.

He held it out in front of him. "The police will want this." With an impatient, almost angry motion, he put the sack on the counter by the sink.

"The police?" Whitney stared at him blankly.

He faced her. "Yes. You've called them, haven't you?"

She glanced away. "No, I—I'm not going to call them."

Frowning, Devlin came to the table where she was sitting. He pulled out a chair directly across from her and straddled it.

Whitney could feel his scrutiny, knew he was waiting for her to meet his eyes.

When she finally looked at him, he searched her face for a moment, then said, "Whitney, Daniel told me about the other night, about what happened to you at the festival."

Whitney averted her head, saying nothing. Only when he reached across the table and touched her hand to get her attention did she once more meet his gaze.

"Daniel said that the man who attacked you was dressed in the costume of a *Pierrot*."

Reluctantly, she nodded, moving her hands to her lap and balling both of them into tight fists.

"Does the *Pierrot* outfit mean anything in particular to you? Is it significant, do you think?"

"What do you mean?" she asked him uneasily, not certain she wanted to hear his answer.

His gaze steady, he replied, "Wasn't *Pierrot* a character in French pantomime?"

"I . . . really don't know," she answered truthfully.

He nodded, seemingly to himself, as he glanced distractedly around her kitchen. "The *mime*, Whitney," he said, shooting her a look of almost fierce meaning. "That's the connection, wouldn't you think? The mime doesn't speak, but simply acts out his desires, his frustrations, from behind a mask of silence."

He hesitated a fraction of a second, then jarred her with the chilling statement, "He knows you, of course."

She flinched, then stiffened.

He went on as if he hadn't noticed. "It would seem to be his idea of a very sick joke, I'd say. By playing the part of a mime, he's actually mocking your deafness."

71

Unshed tears scalded her eyes. Her stomach roiled in response to his words. *Mocking my deafness . . . yes, he always did, in one way or another.*

Devlin's arms had been folded on the back of the chair. He freed them now, resting one hand on each side of the high back as he leaned toward her. "Who is he, Whitney?"

She caught her breath. "What?"

"He knows you. He knows you well. And you know him, too. Don't you?"

She shook her head furiously. *"No!"*

His stare remained level. "I see." After a long moment, he said, "You don't want to talk about it? There's nothing you want to tell me?"

Again she shook her head, unwilling to meet his gaze.

He eased himself off the chair. "Would you like me to call the police for you?"

"No!" She knew her answer was too quick, too frantic. Groping for a remnant of composure, she finished weakly, "I . . . I don't want the police."

He got up, walked around the table, and stood staring down at her, waiting until she looked up at him.

"Why not, Whitney?"

She could almost feel the soft tone of his voice. He didn't understand, of course, *couldn't* understand. Anyone else in a similar situation would have already called the police.

He lifted a questioning brow. "Whitney?"

She was jolted by the unexpected kindness—and understanding—in his eyes.

"All right, then," he said. "I'm sure you have your reasons. But what about Jennifer? Shall I call her, ask her to come over?"

Caught off guard by his unquestioning acceptance, Whitney stammered, "N-no, please. I don't want to bring her . . . and Daniel into this. I—it might cause trouble for them."

Again his look was knowing but gentle. "But they'd want to

help, don't you think?"

When she didn't answer, he pressed. "What about me, Whitney? There must be something I can do."

If only there were. She glanced down at the floor, then looked up at him, shaking her head.

When the lights over the sink began to flash, they both jumped. Whitney pushed herself away from the table and got up. "It's the phone."

Crossing the room to a small table beside the window, she lifted the receiver and said hello, then waited for the answering message to appear on the telecommunications LCD display.

"Whitney? It's Jennifer. Are you all right? I called earlier to make sure you got home okay, but you didn't answer."

Sensing the concern behind Jennifer's inquiry, Whitney quickly reassured her, glancing at Devlin as she spoke.

"I'm . . . fine, Jennifer."

Again the display responded. *"Everything's all right, then?"*

Devlin was leaning up against the counter watching her closely.

"Yes. Yes . . . everything is fine."

"Good. Sleep well. I'll call you tomorrow."

"All right. Goodnight, Jennifer."

After she'd replaced the receiver, Devlin straightened from his slouch and went to stand in front of her. Motioning to the phone, he said, "She's very protective of you, isn't she?"

Immediately defensive, Whitney said sharply, "She's a good friend."

"I wasn't being critical. To the contrary, I find myself liking Jennifer and her remarkable husband very much."

Whitney relaxed. "They've been wonderful to me."

He nodded slowly. "And you're afraid they'll be hurt." His eyes seemed to probe right to the center of her heart. "That's it, isn't it, Whitney? You're afraid that anyone who tries to help

73

you will be hurt."

She backed away from him. "Please, don't . . ."

He lifted a hand, made a short dismissing motion. "It's all right, you don't have to tell me. But at least, let me take that—" he glanced over at the plastic sack on the counter— "let me take it to the police and tell them what's going on."

She shook her head in dismay. "No! I told you . . . "

"Whitney, listen to me."

Even though she couldn't hear his voice, Whitney knew by the way his eyes suddenly flared that his tone was hard and urgent. "You have your reasons for not wanting anyone to know what's happening to you. But you're taking a very foolish and very dangerous risk."

She started to interrupt, but he ignored her. "I can talk to the police, alert them to the fact that you need protection. I can explain your—desire for privacy so that they'll respect it. I understand how their minds work. I used to be one of them, you know."

"But you don't understand . . . "

He was obviously losing the battle for his patience. "I understand," he said, his chin lifting aggressively, "that you have your reasons for not wanting publicity. You made that clear earlier tonight when I suggested getting you some exposure for the Association. And a police investigation—" he shrugged meaningfully— "is seldom kept under wraps from the local newspapers."

He stopped, released a long breath, and crossed his arms over his chest. His expression softened to what might have been compassion. "You have to trust someone, sometime, Whitney."

She bristled, glaring at him. "I trust my God."

He looked at her for a long, tense moment. "I'm sure you do," he finally said, his features now cold and implacable. "I'm simply suggesting that you might want to apply a bit of common sense to your faith."

She flinched at the obvious contempt in his expression.

Anger struggled with humiliation, but she suddenly remembered something she'd seen in his face earlier that evening, when they were leaving the church after the prayer service.

Several members of the congregation had come around to introduce themselves to Devlin. It was then that Whitney had seen his seemingly ironclad composure begin to slip.

The natural, ebullient friendliness of the small church family seemed to throw the lean-faced journalist momentarily off balance. Watching him during that unguarded moment, Whitney had been reminded of an ill-at-ease, lonely adolescent, unable to respond to any semblance of warmth or affection. Devlin actually looked as if he'd like nothing better than to turn and run.

Her irritation with him faded with the memory of that unguarded look of loneliness she had seen in his eyes. Apparently Devlin had built his own wall of self-defense, just as she had.

Sagging with fatigue and defeat, she said, "Do you really think the police will listen to you? That they'd keep it . . . quiet?"

He blinked, moistened his lips, and said hurriedly, "Yes. I really do, Whitney." His eyes willed her to believe him.

She knew he was in no position to offer her that kind of reassurance. But she also admitted to herself that he was at least partially right: She had to use some common sense, take *some* measure of precaution.

So you're admitting that it's Cory . . . .

Of course, it's Cory! It couldn't be anyone else!

But how? They had told her it would be years before he'd be free . . . if ever.

It didn't matter what they'd told her . . . it was him. Cory. As insane, as vicious, as savagely dangerous as ever. He was free . . . and he had found her.

"Whitney?"

75

Numbly, she stared at Devlin, wanting to believe him, needing desperately to trust him.

Finally she whispered, "All right. Yes . . . take it out of here. Please. Just . . . get rid of it."

At the front door, he turned to her. "They connected my phone this morning." Propping the plastic sack by the door for a moment, he pulled a small pad and a pencil from his jacket pocket.

"Here's my number," he told her, scrawling across the top sheet of the pad, then tearing it free and pressing it into her hand. "Memorize it. You can call me anytime—night or day. Count to—fifteen or so—I'll have answered by then." He glanced at the phone on the small desk in the landing. "That display on the phone—can I use that somehow, to call you?"

She shook her head. "You have to have a special code grid that works on the touchtone numbers. It takes a while to get one."

His mouth twisted. "Well, at least you can call me." He looked at her. "You will, won't you?"

She hesitated but finally nodded.

"Remember. You can't hear me, but I can hear you. Just tell me you need me, and I'll come." He picked up the plastic sack and moved to open the door.

Abruptly, he turned back to her, searching her eyes. "That's a promise, Whitney. If you need me, I'll come."

Whitney's throat tightened at the softness, the depth of kindness she encountered in his eyes.

"Tomorrow," he said, reaching for the doorknob, "I'll come by and rig your windows so they won't be so easily opened. That's how he got in, you see. Through that rickety bedroom window in the back. I've got it jammed for now, but I want to do something a bit more permanent to it and the others."

Studying his face, she asked him, "Why are you doing all this for me?"

76

For a moment he looked as if he were going to answer her. Instead, he simply gave her a small, uncertain smile, lifted his shoulders in a somewhat helpless shrug, then turned and opened the door to leave.

The total and immediate chill he left in his wake stunned her. Pressing her face against the cold wood of the door, Whitney squeezed her eyes shut, fighting against the hammering urge to call him back.

Finally, she turned and faced the empty, shadowed living room, forcing herself to accept what had come.

It was on her again, the lonely, nightmare vigil of terror she had thought forever ended. Now would begin the agonizing struggle for courage, the wrenching prayers for strength, the desperate groping for faith enough to survive the fear.

"The Lord is the stronghold of my life . . . of whom shall I be afraid . . . "

But, Father . . . I am afraid . . . forgive me, but I'm so terribly afraid.

8

He stood in the deep shadows of the dingy room, glaring angrily into the darkness.

Finally he moved, flinging his coat and cap over a chair. Then he began to stalk back and forth across the kitchen floor, yanking almost painfully at the knuckles on his hands as he fought down the debilitating rage that lately seemed to hover just beyond the edge of his mind.

This wasn't how he'd planned it. It was never going to work this way. She was supposed to be alone. Completely alone.

His entire plan depended on her vulnerability, her solitary lifestyle. Now it seemed that he was going to have to deal with a bunch of bodyguards before he could go any further.

She had always been one to get herself involved with other people's problems. He would have thought he'd cured her of that, but apparently she needed another lesson.

He dropped down on a hard kitchen chair and, leaning forward, began to massage first one knee, then the other.

Okay, so he'd have to back up and rewrite a couple of scenes. No big deal. All he had to do was get rid of the extras.

He'd do it one at a time.

His frown changed to a smile. He'd start with the Kaines, since they seemed to be so tight with their new little friend.

The blind man first. He'd be the easiest. He nodded to himself. Sure, he'd start with Kaine.

Abruptly, he hauled himself to his feet. Easing into a set of tension-relieving exercises, he continued to plan.

Yeah, it made sense to take Kaine out of the picture first. Even blind, a giant like that one could be trouble. He looked as if he'd have the strength of three men.

But he'd be a pushover for an accident.

After a few minutes, he started to perspire, so he ceased the exercises. Walking over to the window, he stared out into the thick, silent darkness, thinking.

What would be the best way to put Kaine out of business? He'd have to be careful. A handicapped guy running a radio station in a small burg like this—he'd be well-known. Anything suspicious with a blind man, and the cops would be all over it, shaking it to death.

No, it couldn't be anything obvious. After a moment, he smiled again, returning to the idea of an accident. Sure, that was the way to go. Blind people were just naturally accident-prone, weren't they?

But where? He would have to get Kaine alone, without the guide dog. And from what he'd seen, that wouldn't be easy. The dog seemed to go anywhere the blind man went.

A dog like that would be smart, too. Highly trained. He shook his head. It'd be considerably easier if he could get Kaine by himself.

Shrugging, he turned away from the window, his eyes roaming over the shadows of the room. He'd work it out. The thing to do was to come up with a plan that had a chance of getting by the dog, just in case he couldn't isolate the blind man.

If it didn't work—he shrugged again—he'd go to Plan B.

Feeling good now—loose and confident and powerful—he flexed his shoulder muscles a couple of times and started toward the bedroom.

There was just enough moonlight filtering through the

window to let him find the suitcase at the foot of the bed. He stooped to open it, fumbling through the neatly folded stacks until he found some clean clothes and his manicure set.

He straightened, running a hand over his face, then passing it through his hair. He'd wash up and get some sleep. In the morning, he'd be fresher, better able to work out a plan for Kaine. Something for tomorrow night, hopefully. He didn't want to stay in one place any longer than he had to. The sooner he got rid of all the yokels running interference for Whitney, the sooner he could make his move on her, take her out of this Hick City.

He nodded decisively, tucking the clothes and the manicure kit under his arm. Then, pursing his lips in a soft whistle, he turned and left the room.

9

"Hadn't we better get out of here, Daniel? It's almost ten o'clock, and we still have to pick up Jason at your mother's."

Jennifer's last few words were half-swallowed by an enormous yawn. Then she went on. "Come on, boss, give it a rest. This is the second night this week we've worked late. We're going to get another lecture from your dad about stress if we don't watch it."

"As if he's ever put in a normal eight hour day in his life." Daniel stood up from his desk and stretched his arms above his head, groaning at the stiffness in his shoulders.

"But as Lucas would remind you, *he's* a doctor."

"Right. And, as we both know—"

"—you don't go into medicine if you want a nine-to-five day," they chimed in singsong unison, echoing Lucas Kaine's automatic reply when Daniel's mother scolded him for working too hard.

Daniel touched the face of his Braille watch. "We should have told Mom that Jason could spend the night when she asked since tomorrow's Saturday."

"He just spent last weekend with Gabe and Lyss. The child spends as much time with your family as he does at home."

Picking up a handful of Braille programming charts, Daniel thumped them on the work table a few times to make a stack. "It's good for him. He had almost eight years in the Children's Home with no family. Let him enjoy what he's got," he said firmly.

Jennifer walked around the table to where he was

standing. "I'd never tell him so, but Gabe is sorely missed around here. The work load is nearly double without him." She took the charts from Daniel, saying, "This is the last batch. I'll put them in my office with the others."

Daniel caught her by the waist. "Suppose you could stop being efficient long enough to hug your husband?"

"I get paid for being efficient."

"But you're on overtime," he told her, taking the charts out of her hand and returning them to the table. "And since you don't get paid for overtime—"

"—don't I know it?"

"—you might just as well relax."

As always, she came into his arms with a soft little laugh, smelling like sunshine and warming his heart with the love he could feel shining out from her.

He kissed her.

"Mm. My kind of hug," she said, the smile in her voice still intact.

He buried his face in her hair, delighting himself in the weight of it, the dizzying, fresh scent of it. "I love you, kid. Or have I already told you that today?"

"You might want to run it by me again in case I missed it the first few times."

He held her close for a long moment, then kissed her again.

At her sigh, he lifted a brow and asked, "What's that for?"

She eased back, but stayed within the circle of his arms. "Did I tell you about my conversation with Whitney this afternoon?"

"No. But you're going to, right?"

"I am *so* worried about her, Daniel. She sounded very— *strange* on the phone."

"Strange? How?"

Her answer came without hesitation. "Evasive. She sounded evasive. And what *really* upsets me—she's having

82

dinner with Michael Devlin tomorrow night."

He smiled at the pique in her tone. "I think that's perfectly acceptable behavior for two single adults, Jennifer."

"She doesn't *know* him."

He shrugged. "That's what dating is about, isn't it? Getting to know one another?"

"It's different with Whitney."

"How is it different with Whitney?" he asked patiently.

"Because of what happened to her the other night, Daniel!" she snapped. "For goodness' sake, she was *attacked.* In an alley!"

He nodded slowly. He really *did* understand her concern. And he knew his wife well enough to know there was no freeing her of it. To some extent, he shared Jennifer's protective instincts toward Whitney Sharyn, but what he *didn't* share was her distrust of Devlin.

"Look at it this way, Jennifer. Dev might be a good man to have around in case of trouble. You're talking about a guy who's probably been face-to-face with every kind of crisis situation imaginable, even terrorism. Maybe it wouldn't be such a bad thing if he and Whitney started spending time together."

"You *like* him," she said flatly, as if that explained the aberration in his reasoning.

"Let's not start on that," he warned, tightening his hands around her waist.

Again she sighed, and he knew the conversation was a standoff. Brushing a quick kiss across her forehead, he turned to gather up the charts. "Do what you must with these," he said, handing them back to her, "and let's get out of here."

He followed her to the door of the office. "How long are you going to be?"

"Just a few minutes. I want to put the charts away and clear off my desk."

He yawned again. "I'm going to stick my head out the door

83

and get some air." He turned back, in the direction of his desk. "Sunny, you can stay. I'll be right back."

The night felt good. For the first time in over a week, the mercury had climbed well above freezing. The station sat at the top of one of the highest hills in the area, so there was always a breeze; tonight, however, the air was unusually mild.

Daniel stood just outside the door, on the small concrete porch, breathing in the scent of woodsmoke and spruce. He smiled with satisfaction at the sound of the encircling oaks and sugar maples whispering to each other amidst the soft scratching of fallen leaves.

It was his favorite time of the year, always had been. Like the grandfather for whom he'd been named, Daniel loved the mountains, had never had the slightest desire to live anywhere else but among them.

"The Lord made everything beautiful in its own time, Danny-Boy," his grandfather had more than once remarked. "But to my way of thinking, He made these mountains beautiful *all* the time."

An active man until the day he died, his grandfather had had a favorite sport or event for each season. Again, Daniel smiled a little at the undeniable similarity in their natures. Like his grandfather, he liked to be moving. Skiing and ice skating in the winter, climbing or whitewater rafting in the summer, horseback riding and hiking in the fall.

His blindness had slowed him down some, but mostly he still did what he wanted to do. Skiing was the exception. There was something about racing down a mountain into the vast unknown that he simply couldn't handle.

A new thought struck him, and again he grinned as he walked across the square concrete porch.

Wouldn't Grandpa Dan have taken a shine to Jennifer, though? The old man's stubbornness and Jennifer's feistiness would have been something to behold. The two of them would have scrapped from sunup to sundown, with

Grandpa loving every fiery minute of it. And loving Jennifer at the same time. Oh yes, he surely would have loved her.

His grin softened to a smile of tenderness. *She's an easy lady to love, my wife* ... That honey-voiced rebel had had his heart doing kneebends since the first day she'd crashed into his life. He lost his smile as he shoved his hands into his pockets and lifted his face, letting the night air wash over him.

If only she weren't such a mother-hen...

Not that she'd ever change. At least, he doubted it. The pattern for Jennifer's oversized caring heart had been shaped years ago. When her mother died, she'd been a big sister to two younger brothers. He knew her father, a high school band director, had taken on private students during evenings and weekends to help pay the outrageous medical bills left over from his wife's illness. Although Jennifer would never have admitted it—probably, she had never even realized it—Daniel knew his wife had sacrificed a great deal in her determination to take as much pressure as she possibly could off her father's sagging shoulders.

That kind of responsibility thrust upon a 16-year-old girl, in combination with her natural protective instincts, had most likely set the continuing theme for Jennifer's life. She was fiercely defensive of those she loved—now he could smile again—and couldn't seem to help trying to manage their lives.

And he loved her for it. *Oh, dear Lord, how I love her . . . . I'll praise you and thank you every day of my life for giving me this woman to love.*

Still smiling, he freed one hand, felt for the wrought iron railing by the steps and started down.

A sharp, stunned cry of alarm exploded from him as he pitched forward, his right foot trapped at the ankle by something thin and tight. With his right hand, he grabbed for the railing, finding nothing but air.

He groped desperately for the touch of wrought iron on

either side, but it was too late. He shot out over the steps, crashing onto the concrete walk at the bottom. His right leg buckled under him, snapping so fast and hard he screamed in agony.

The pain was a blast of scalding water, seizing him and sucking him under into a boiling whirlpool that sent shock waves raging through his entire body. He shouted again, but most of the sound was trapped by a sudden onslaught of weakness.

He tried to raise himself off his leg but fell forward at the effort. Now fighting the clutch of nausea, he called Jennifer's name with as much strength as he could muster, knowing even as he cried out how unlikely it was that she would hear him.

At the door to her office, Jennifer put a hand to the light switch, paused, then turned to glance back at the charts now neatly stacked on the work table near the desk. After an instant she sighed with tired satisfaction, turned off the overhead light, and closed the door.

Crossing the hall, she heard Sunny bark once, then again, louder.

She began to talk to her before she reached the door to Daniel's office. "Yes, I know, girl," she said conversationally. "He forgot about us again. Most likely he's out there hugging a tree or talking to the moon or whatever the man does when he disappears after dark. Why don't we just go ahead and lock up? Then we'll track him down, okay?"

But when she entered the office, there was no sign of the retriever. Puzzled, she went to look behind the desk, frowning when she didn't find the dog. It wasn't like Sunny to disobey Daniel. When the retriever was told to stay, she stayed. Always.

Jennifer whirled around in surprise at the sound of Sunny's furious barking. Staring blankly at the open door for an instant, she finally moved, bolting from the office and half-running down the hall.

She stopped short when she reached the receptionist's desk, bewildered by the sight of an obviously agitated Sunny. The dog was prancing back and forth in front of the double entrance doors, no longer barking, but now whining, then snarling with apparent frustration.

As soon as the retriever saw Jennifer, she bounded toward her, her desperate barking renewed.

Bending over, Jennifer put a hand on the dog's head to try to soothe her. "What's the matter, girl? What is it?"

Sunny wouldn't stand still, but with an air of anxiety turned in the direction of the door, then back to Jennifer.

Unaccustomed to this type of behavior from the highly trained guide dog, Jennifer again puzzled over what the retriever was trying to tell her. "Sunny? What do you want, girl?" she asked as she straightened.

The dog dashed to the door, turned to Jennifer and barked savagely.

Something was wrong. Sunny wouldn't carry on this way for no reason. Even when she desperately needed to go outside, she would merely assume a patient, waiting stance beside the door until someone took notice of her.

As if to berate Jennifer for her hesitation, the dog turned frenzied, dark eyes in her direction and barked fiercely.

Swallowing down the sudden dryness in her mouth, Jennifer finally moved. Whatever had the dog so upset was obviously outside.

"Daniel!"

She charged for the door, flinging both sides open with a force that sent them banging against the wall. The retriever slipped by her like a golden streak and bolted across the porch, looking back only once more to make sure Jennifer was following.

Jennifer cried Daniel's name again, a startled scream of horror at the sight of him lying prostrate on the concrete walk, bent and huddled in obvious agony.

10

Stepping back from the examining table, Lucas Kaine crossed his arms over his chest and surveyed his efforts with a clinical eye. The completed cast covered a little over half of Daniel's right leg.

"I'm going to admit you for the rest of the night," he said. Clearly anticipating a challenge from his son, he added, "It's almost 2:00 now. I want your circulation monitored for the next few hours. We'll get you released before noon if everything looks all right."

With a distracted glance down the splattered front of his blue scrub suit, he headed for the sink in the corner of the room and began to clean the plaster of Paris from his hands and arms.

Now that she could finally move in closer to Daniel, Jennifer clung tightly to his hand, closely studying his face for any lingering signs of pain. She saw that his complexion wasn't quite as pasty as it had been when the medics had first brought him in on the cart. Still, she felt a pang of concern at the drawn, haggard set of his features.

"How long, Dad?" Daniel's voice was quiet, but edged with an unmistakable note of apprehension. "How long will I have to wear this—thing?"

Lucas slowly turned around, wiping his hands on a white hospital towel as he came to stand at the foot of the examining table.

Watching him, Jennifer was struck again by the marked resemblance between Daniel and his father. A big man, Lucas Kaine's size was still less formidable than that of his son. Both men, however, had the same incredibly deep blue eyes, the same high, prominent cheekbones, and the same rather arrogant, hawkish nose that Daniel's sister, Lyss, often referred to as the "mark of Kaine."

Lucas smoothed his thick silver hair with one hand as he quietly studied his son's face. With obvious reluctance, he finally answered Daniel. "Too long to suit you, I expect. It'll be a few weeks before we can put you in a walking cast."

"A few *weeks*?" With a stunned, incredulous expression, Daniel pushed himself up on his elbows. "I'm going to be laid up for *weeks*? Come on, Dad—I broke my *leg*, not my back!"

"Daniel," Lucas began patiently, glancing at Jennifer as he spoke, "you broke your shinbone. A broken bone takes time to mend. Time in a *cast*. And—" he continued forcefully over Daniel's attempted interruption—"it is also going to take your full cooperation."

With a mournful groan that squeezed Jennifer's heart, Daniel fell back onto the table.

Exchanging looks with Lucas, Jennifer felt certain they were both concerned about the same thing. This unexpected curtailment of activity would increase the burden of Daniel's blindness.

Her throat tightening with despair, she glanced away. For a moment, her gaze roamed the aging examining room with its faded white paint and outdated fixtures. It was, she decided, a drab, depressing room.

Letting out a long breath, she turned back to Daniel, determined to sound a lot more cheerful than she felt. "It won't be so bad, Daniel," she said, her words spilling out in a rush as she bent over him. "You'll probably be able to go back to work in a few days." She shot a questioning glance at her father-in-law.

When Lucas merely lifted his brows and inclined his head in an expression of uncertainty, Jennifer scrambled to think of some small scrap of reassurance to offer her husband.

"What we have to do, Daniel, is just—keep busy. And there are lots of things you can do at home. You can work on the ensemble music for the teens . . . and you have some new books on tape you haven't had time to listen to yet. And, Daniel, this would be a perfect time to start getting some notes together for that workshop we're going to be doing next spring in Kentucky, the one Mitch wrote to you about."

He didn't answer. His face appeared to be set in a scowl as firm as the cast on his leg.

As if to give her efforts a boost, Lucas interjected a hopeful note of his own. "You'll be able to get around on crutches in a few days, son. This is going to slow you down a little, true, but it's not as if you'll be totally immobile."

Jennifer gave her father-in-law a grateful smile and squeezed Daniel's hand. "Cheer up, darling. Please."

He turned his face toward her and finally, with obvious effort, managed a smile and a small nod. "I'm okay. Just tired."

"You need to rest," Lucas agreed, "but Rick Hill is still out in the waiting room. I promised you'd talk with him after we got the cast on."

"Who called the police?" Daniel asked with no real show of interest.

"The ward secretary," his father replied. "Mary Ryan called me out of CCU to talk with Jennifer when she called, and when I hung up, I asked Mary to call the squad and the police while I changed into my scrubs."

"We were talking just tonight about your long hours, Lucas," Jennifer told him. "For once, I'm glad you *weren't* at home."

"Pauline says I never am." He grinned at Jennifer and said, "Listen, I'm going to change before this plaster sets up and I have to wear these scrubs forever. Okay if I send Rick in on my way out?"

Daniel nodded. "I can't tell him much, but let him come in."

Lucas started toward the door, then turned back to Jennifer. "Where's Jason? Is he still at our house?"

"Yes. We were just getting ready to leave the station and come after him when—"

He nodded, making it unnecessary for her to finish. "I suppose you intend to spend the rest of the night here, too?"

"Yes," she said firmly, before Daniel had a chance to object. "When I called Pauline to tell her about Daniel, she said she'd already put Jason to bed."

Again Lucas nodded. "All right. I'll look in before I leave for home." Glancing once more at his son, he told him, "They'll get you settled in a private room as soon as you've talked with Rick, Daniel. And I'll leave instructions for pain medication over the next few hours. Just tell one of the nurses when you need it."

The uniformed patrolman who entered the examining room after Lucas left was young, fair-haired, and, she knew, extremely capable.

Holding his cap under one arm, he greeted Jennifer, then went to stand beside Daniel at the examining table.

"Dan. Sorry to hear about this." He pulled a small notebook from his pocket. "Can you tell me anything that will help?"

Daniel smiled grimly and rubbed a hand down his beard. "Dad said you went to the station before you came here?"

The officer nodded. "Right. I wanted to see that piece of wire across the step before it was taken down."

He paused, glancing at Jennifer. "You were inside the station when it happened, weren't you, Mrs. Kaine?"

"Yes. Daniel had gone out on the porch to get some air," she explained. "I was just getting ready to lock up when I heard Sunny going crazy in the lobby."

"You left Sunny inside, Dan?" The officer glanced across the examining table to the retriever sitting alertly at Daniel's

91

side. Her ears had pricked at the sound of her name, and she cocked her head at the policeman.

Daniel nodded. "I hadn't planned to stay more than a couple of minutes."

"Did you hear anything at all while you were outside?" the patrolman asked, frowning as he studied the cumbersome cast on Daniel's leg.

Daniel shook his head. "Nothing but the wind pushing the leaves around. Someone could have been out there, I suppose, but I didn't hear anything."

"Rick—"

The officer looked at Jennifer, waiting.

"I don't think anyone was around. Sunny would have sensed it, and she never budged from Daniel's side once we got outside."

Nodding at Jennifer's logic, the patrolman wrote something down in his notebook, then said, "Nothing unusual happened around the station today? No peculiar phone calls or anything like that?"

Again, Daniel shook his head. "Not that I'm aware of."

Jennifer agreed. "Nothing."

Pushing the notebook back into his pocket, the officer looked from Jennifer to Daniel. "Well—it's not much, but we'll do what we can."

"What kind of wire was it, do you know?" Daniel asked.

"Not yet. It's thin, flexible—it looks to me like the stuff my wife uses in the craft shop, but I'm not sure." He paused, then added thoughtfully, "It's thin enough that it would be hard to see, especially at night. I'm not so sure even your dog would have spotted it, Dan."

His expression glum, Daniel shook his head with conviction. "Sunny would have spotted it. I wouldn't be in this mess if I'd just taken her outside with me."

The officer's look was sympathetic. "Well, I'll get back to you as soon as I know more about it."

He took a step away from the table, then turned back. "Dan, what's your feeling about this? Any ideas who might be responsible?"

Daniel frowned, then shook his head. "I'm afraid not. It doesn't make any sense to me."

"Mrs. Kaine?"

Jennifer shook her head in frustration, looking at Daniel, then at the policeman. Throughout the entire time that Lucas and the nurse had been working on Daniel's cast, she'd raked her mind for even a hint as to what kind of a person would be vicious enough to do such a thing to a man who couldn't see.

"I can't imagine who—or *why*," she replied, her voice trembling with anger and helplessness. "Only a sick mind would think of a stunt like this."

Rick Hill gave both of them a compassionate glance before starting for the door. "If you happen to think of anything that might be important, just give us a call. Dan— take care. I'll be in touch." He stopped. "How's Miss Sharyn doing, by the way?" he asked, looking at Jennifer. "No more trouble since the night of the Festival, I hope?"

"No, she's just fine," Jennifer answered with a smile, knowing Officer Hill had been one of the patrolmen who talked with Whitney the night she was attacked. "I'll tell her you asked about her."

He nodded, putting on his cap as he went out the door.

Jennifer continued to grip Daniel's hand, neither of them saying anything for a long moment. Finally, she bent over and brushed a gentle kiss across his forehead. "Are you feeling terrible, Daniel?"

His attempted smile failed, but he managed a weak shake of the head. "Probably not the way you mean."

Puzzled, she frowned. "What?"

He squeezed his eyes shut, then opened them. "This is going to be the pits, Jennifer. For both of us."

"Daniel—"

He pulled his hand away. "Just . . . see if they've got a room ready for me yet, would you? I'm beat."

Bewildered, she studied his face with new concern, wishing Lucas would come back.

"Jennifer?"

"All right, I'll—go check on your room. Would you like me to see about some pain medication, too, Daniel? I think you ought to have—"

"Just a bed," he said shortly. "And, Jennifer—*please* don't start . . . hovering. I don't need a private nurse. I just need some sleep."

Stung by his sharpness, Jennifer blinked back tears of hurt as she moved away from the examining table.

Of course, he didn't mean it, she told herself all the way out the door and down the hall. He was in pain; he was exhausted, and he had been through a terrible experience. Who *wouldn't* be impatient and cross?

Spying Lucas at the nurse's station at the far end of the hall, she pulled in a deep breath and began to walk a little faster.

She was simply going to have to be patient with Daniel. He'd be fine in a few days; she'd see to it. She wouldn't hover, though. She knew Daniel hated to be *smothered.* It had been one of his biggest frustrations in the months following the accident that had blinded him. The over-protective attitudes of his family and friends had made it impossible to have any privacy, he'd told her. Everyone had made such a business of protecting him that they had very nearly *suffocated* him.

No, she again told herself firmly, *I am* not *going to hover.* Obviously, he was already expecting her to do just that. Well, she would surprise him.

She would.

11

Devlin pulled in at the curb, put the Bronco in park, and let the motor idle. Turning the heater fan to low, he cut the headlights and switched on his parking lights and interior lights. The windshield wipers continued to thump, spreading the driving rain into scattered sheets across the glass.

"Nice night," he said with a cynical lift of one eyebrow.

Whitney smiled at his expression, then glanced out the front windshield. There was nothing to be seen except a distorted splash of asphalt.

"I'm afraid I'm one of those odd people who likes the rain," she confessed. "When I was little, I used to sneak outside late at night when it was raining and just sit on the porch and watch." Turning back to him, she asked, "Does it rain a lot in Ireland? Is that what's responsible for the 'emerald hills' and 'shamrock fields'?"

He was leaning back, an arm draped comfortably across the top of the seat, his head turned toward her. There was the faintest hint of a smile in his eyes, and his features gentled even more as he studied her face. Suddenly, he laughed, and Whitney was once again jolted by the unexpected transformation. Without the grim, hard set to his mouth and the brooding darkness in his eyes, he looked years younger.

"I wouldn't want to shatter your image of the land, but I'm afraid it's not as green and golden as you may have read." He looked away for a moment, then back. His expression changed abruptly as he added, "These days our hills and fields are running red."

So strong was the bitter sorrow in his expression that

Whitney felt as if he had touched her. "Is that why you left?" she asked hesitantly. "Because of the violence?"

His eyes turned bleak as he looked, not at her, but into the darkness beyond the window on her side. "In a way, yes." For a long moment, he seemed to stare at something in his past. Then he blinked, regarding her as if he'd only then remembered her presence.

Pain. She could see it in him. A terrible pain, gnawing at him, aging him . . . eroding him.

"Do you think . . . you'll ever go back?" she asked him softly.

If she thought she had seen pain before, she instinctively drew away from the raw anguish now glistening in his eyes. The hand resting on the steering wheel tightened, clenching the rim in a white-knuckled grasp. For one irrational moment, Whitney wanted to touch him, a touch of comfort. She balled her own hand into a tight fist to resist the impulse.

"It's hard to say," Devlin finally answered, shaking his head as he spoke. "I'm an American citizen now. I don't think I'd ever go back."

"You're a citizen? I didn't realize you'd been here that long."

When he made no reply, she said, "Still, you'd want to go back to visit someday, wouldn't you?"

He looked at her, shrugging in an apparent attempt at indifference. "I've no one to visit."

Whitney found it unsettling to realize how little she knew about this man—and how much she wanted to know. He continued to slip in and out of her days, puzzling her with his questions, his apparent interest in her, and his multifaceted personality that seemed to have no end to its contrasts and contradictions.

Just as he'd promised, he had shown up on Thursday to secure her windows with a simple crossed nail gimmick. He'd grumbled and grouched most of the time he was there about the locks on the front office door and the one on the connecting door to her apartment, demanding a promise from her that she'd have both replaced as soon as possible. Then, in almost the same breath, he'd flashed that short-circuiting smile of his and asked her to dinner.

It could easily have been an evening to turn her head, had Devlin behaved more as an interested suitor and less like a journalist. Not, she had hastily reminded herself, that she was ready to think of any man in that way. Certainly not now . . . perhaps not ever.

Still, the evening had held a heady, distracting atmosphere. Joe Como had treated them to a small, private dining room, subtly romantic with candlelight and, Devlin had informed her, "weeping violins" in the background.

Sitting across the small table from the enigmatic Irishman, watching the candlelight shadows play over his face as he concentrated the total force of his attention on her, it would have been all too easy to forget her resolve to keep things impersonal.

Devlin, however, made it entirely possible for her to maintain a safe emotional distance. For over two hours, Whitney felt as if she were being *interviewed,* not courted—interviewed by a smooth professional with the formidable combination of a journalist's technique and a policeman's authority.

Frequently during the evening, she had felt herself caught in an almost painful grip of tension, brought on by the continued effort to stay one step ahead of Devlin's skillful, sharply arrowed questions.

At one point, irritated and unsettled by what she was beginning to think bordered on an invasion of privacy, Whitney had shot him a frosty look and snapped, "Are you writing a book, Mr. Devlin?"

He blinked and grinned, apparently unruffled by her peevishness. "Michael," he corrected automatically. Without

97

missing a beat, he immediately skated into another question about her background.

Her exasperation with him ebbed later as they sat in his car and he apologized. "I'm afraid I forget how wholly obnoxious an ex-cop turned journalist can be to a normal person like yourself. I suppose I've been acting like a wolfhound worrying a bone."

"As a matter of fact," Whitney told him with exaggerated sweetness, "you have."

"Old habits die hard, you see," he said with an apologetic smile.

She was fairly certain that she'd told him no more than she wanted him to know. Certainly, she knew little more about *him* than she had at the beginning of the evening.

Stubbornly, she decided to try a different route of her own questioning. "I'm afraid the only thing I know about Belfast is that the Titanic was built there," she said, hoping to focus the conversation on him.

He nodded. "There's little else worth knowing about Belfast."

"You don't sound overly fond of your home."

He looked at her as if he were about to object to something she'd said. Then his expression took on the familiar fixed mask. "It's difficult for me to be fond of Belfast. She's a sour old city: somber, rather dismal, and not especially hospitable. It has something to do with bombs being tossed back and forth in the streets and children being murdered in their schoolyards, I suspect."

His always hard jawline seemed to be cut from stone.

"It must have been extremely ... difficult to be a policeman in those surroundings."

His eyes turned bitter. "You can't be a policeman in Belfast. You can be a warrior or a terrorist or a soldier or a killer. But you can't possibly be a policeman." He stopped. His next words came slowly, and seemed to be directed to himself. "A policeman is meant to be a keeper of the peace, you see. But in Belfast, there has never been any peace to keep. The entire city is a battleground, and peace is only spoken of at funerals."

With a clear attempt at changing the subject, he peered around her head in the direction of her house, now totally obscured by the night and the curtain of rain washing down the window on her side. "This is a wonderful neighborhood, you know. I'll most likely use a shameful amount of film on it. It's a remarkable town, isn't it? Few things fit the word *quaint* any longer, but Shepherd Valley would seem to wear the word well."

Whitney nodded in agreement, once more feeling her balance tilt as she watched his dour mood change to an almost boyish enthusiasm. "I love it here. I hope . . . I never have to leave."

His gaze roamed her face, his mouth softening to a smile. "Yes, I would have imagined you to be one for home and hearthfire, Whitney Sharyn."

She suddenly found herself wishing she could hear his voice, listen to him say her name. She thought his words would glide and flow with rhythm; somehow she knew his voice would be melodic, low-pitched with an easy lilt. He smiled again, his eyes twinkling with a look of affection so warm she lost her breath at it.

Their gazes locked until it became awkward. It was Devlin who broke the moment. He stirred, dropped his arm from the back of the seat, and said, "I suppose we should be getting you inside. The rain's eased a bit."

He turned off the lights and pulled his keys from the ignition, then opened the door on his side and got out.

The earlier drenching downpour had diminished to a steady, lighter rain. As soon as Michael helped her out of the car, they bolted up the steps and through the gate, then took off running down the walk until, laughing, they reached the back porch.

Whitney had a raincoat on, but Michael had taken the

worst of it in his corduroy sportcoat. His eyes locked with hers as he extended his hand for her key.

She watched him fit the key into the lock. Abruptly, he turned, catching her off guard. His rain-satined hair had begun to curl at the ends, and his eyes were dancing with laughter. Pushing the door open with one hand, he watched her until she made herself brush by him and go inside.

In the landing, she turned, expecting to say goodnight. Instead, Michael stepped inside, clearly feeling no need for an invitation.

"I'll have a look through the house before I leave," he said, wiping his feet on the floor mat.

"No . . . I mean, that's not necessary."

"I'd feel better," he replied, his glance going from her face to the wall switch at his side. He reached for it, flipped it on.

"Michael . . . I can't have someone following me into the house every time I come home after dark," she said, frowning up at him.

"You can if I'm the one who brings you home," he replied with a deceptively bland look.

"But—"

"You'd best get out of that raincoat," he said, already heading for the living room.

Ignoring his suggestion, Whitney went to the doorway, waiting until he found the table lamp and turned it on.

She started to follow him through the room, but he turned and said, "No. Wait here for me."

He suddenly seemed very tall, taking up a surprising amount of space. Annoyed by his smooth assumption of command, Whitney let the hood of her raincoat fall around her neck as she glared at him. Lifting her chin, Whitney demanded, "Did someone . . . hire you as my bodyguard and forget to tell me about it?"

Now he grinned openly. "Not at all. What it is, you see, is that I got a bit bored, being away from the force and all. So I appointed myself as your personal—escort."

"An escort's responsibilities," Whitney said slowly and pointedly, "end at the door, I believe."

His eyes went over her face. Still smiling, he sighed. "More the pity."

He turned then, leaving Whitney to stare at his back as he started off toward the breakfast nook. Drawing in a long breath, she at first tried to tell herself she was irritated because she'd allowed him to dictate to her. The truth was, she admitted after a moment, that she was angry with *herself* because of the overwhelming sense of relief she'd felt when he insisted on coming inside with her.

Returning to the entrance hall, she set her purse on the desk, then hung up her raincoat. She fluffed her hair with her fingers to shake off the dampness, then remembered that she hadn't talked with Jennifer today. She'd tried the house unsuccessfully several times through the afternoon. Not that they managed to talk every day. Still, it was common for them to have what Jennifer called "week-in-review" phone chats on Saturday afternoons, since neither of them usually worked past one or two o'clock that day.

She glanced at her watch. Almost 10:00. Even if— *Michael*—were to leave within the next few minutes, she couldn't call Jennifer this late. They'd have to talk at church in the morning.

Walking back into the living room, she stopped at the thermostat just inside the door to turn up the furnace.

After a short time, Devlin returned. "All seems normal," he announced. Then, "Where's the key for the office? I'll have a look in there as well."

"Oh, really, that's not—"

"It won't take but a moment," he interrupted. "The key?"

Whitney went to fish the key out of her purse. Returning, she slapped it into the palm of his hand a little too firmly.

His gaze skimmed her face. Then he winked at her and

started down the hallway to the office.

This time, she went with him. When she tried to squeeze through the door ahead of him, he sighed. Gently but firmly, he clasped both her shoulders and set her behind him.

The office was uninvitingly cold, but apparently in order. Michael gave the room an efficient, sharp-eyed sweep, his gaze coming to rest on a small milk glass lamp on the credenza behind Whitney's desk.

Whitney watched as he glanced from the lamp to the front window.

"Do you use that lamp?" he asked abruptly, looking down at her.

"Use it?"

"Could we move it?"

"Move it where?"

"There," he said, inclining his head toward the large front window.

He turned back to her. "I want you to do something for me, just to ease my mind a bit."

"What?"

"Let's put the lamp in the window. Put a dim bulb in it, and let it burn at night. Would you do that for me?"

She tilted her head, staring at him as if he'd grown an extra ear.

"Humor me, would you? I can see just the front of the house from my place, no more. So long as I find the lamp burning, I'll know everything's all right with you. If it should happen to go out, that will be our signal that you need help."

Whitney lifted her chin. "Are you serious?"

"Entirely," he replied with a steady look.

"I don't think—"

"You don't mind? Good." He crossed the room, lifted the lamp, and took it to the window, setting it squarely in the middle of the sill. Plugging the cord into the outlet below the window, he straightened and pushed in the small button switch. "That's a bit bright, but it will do for now. You can change the bulb tomorrow."

He scanned the office once more, then, seemingly satisfied, turned out the light. Locking the door behind them as they left the room, he took Whitney by the elbow and crossed the hall to the landing.

He stopped when they reached the outside door, but continued to hold her arm.

"I talked with the police," he said bluntly.

Startled, her head shot up.

He gave a small nod, releasing her arm as he said, "Yes. This afternoon. I simply pressed them for additional protection for you because of last week's attack. I explained that you're being harassed and that you think you're being watched." He stopped, studying her face as if to judge her reaction before going on. "There'll be someone by tomorrow to talk with you, to get some more information."

"You see, I *told* you—"

He stopped her with a stern look and a shake of his head. "Anything you divulge will be held in absolute confidence," he reassured her. "I explained your desire to avoid publicity, and they've agreed to it." He paused, then added, "Whitney, you're going to have to tell them more than you've told me, you know. They can't help you if you don't tell them the truth. All of it."

"It will only make it worse!"

He grasped her by the shoulders almost roughly, his eyes burning into hers. "Whitney—it's time to ask for help, can't you see that? You won't trust me; you don't trust the police— you won't even bring Daniel and Jennifer into your confidence for fear they'll be hurt!"

Stunned by his outburst, Whitney went limp under his hands.

As if he'd only then realized that he might be hurting her, his gaze suddenly cleared and he dropped his hands away from her shoulders. "I'm sorry." He searched her smoke-blue eyes. "I'm sorry, Whitney. I only want to make you see that you have to protect yourself. You wrap yourself up in everyone else's life, pour yourself out for every stray that walks into your world, but you won't lift a finger to ask for help for yourself."

He was staring at her with genuine puzzlement, and Whitney again had the dizzying sensation that this man knew her as well as she knew herself. The thought struck her, chilled her, then fled.

She didn't know what to say to him. She could only stand and stare down at the floor, anything to avoid his piercing, probing gaze.

But he wasn't finished. Tilting her face upward with one finger, he held her captive with his eyes. "You think I don't understand. But I do. You're putting yourself at this madman's mercy because you're afraid of someone else getting hurt. That's what happened before, isn't it? Yes, and now you're afraid it will happen again."

When she tried to turn away without answering, he cupped her chin, forcing her to look at him. "That's it, isn't it, Whitney?"

She remained silent, and he nodded, slowly, knowingly. "You're going to say nothing. You're going to watch for a chance, and then you're going to run."

He scowled down at her, his expression urgent. "Whitney, you can't outrun this lunatic! Face it! He'll find you. Anywhere you go, he'll find you. You've got to stay and fight, don't you see? Get some help and fight him. For once, you're going to have to take instead of give. Ask for help, Whitney. Just—ask for help." He paused, touched her cheek with his fingertips, and said, "Ask me, lass."

Whitney bit her lip to keep from crying out. Trembling, she swallowed against a swelling knot of apprehension.

"Who are you?" she whispered fiercely.

"What?" His eyes narrowed.

"Who *are* you?" she rasped again. "You come crashing into my life, telling me what I need to do—*demanding* that I do what *you* say—as if you have a right! I want to know just who you think you are!"

The question hung between them for a long, silent moment. Finally, with a strange, weary look of resignation, he again skimmed her cheek with his fingertips. Immediately, he dropped his hand away, back to his side.

Never taking his eyes from her face, he said, "I'm your shadow, lass. From now on, until this is over, I'm going to be your shadow."

Giving her no chance to answer, he turned, opened the door, and walked out into the rainy night, leaving her question still unanswered.

She closed the door, locked it, then pressed her face weakly against it. Squeezing her eyes shut, she groped for the strength to withstand her warring emotions.

I'm going to be your shadow . . . .

From the beginning, from the first moment she'd suspected that Cory had somehow managed to get free, she had been intent upon keeping Daniel and Jennifer at arm's length—for their own protection.

During all that time, she hadn't once thought of the threat to Michael Devlin. Before she'd realized what was happening—and what it could ultimately mean to the Irish journalist—he had wedged himself into her life, becoming a part of it, even . . . important to it.

With a sick clutch of despair, she realized that the circle of people around her who could be hurt because of her had grown. Now it included not only Jennifer and Daniel, even Jason, but also Michael Devlin.

Pushing away from the door, she walked over to the desk and stood staring down at it. Her hands gripped the back of the chair tightly.

Why had she ever tried to delude herself into thinking she

had a choice? Even if Michael had only been baiting her about running away, he was right. She couldn't possibly stay here.

But, dear Lord, how do I bring myself to leave? I love this place . . . the town, my job, the people . . . I love it all—so much. Do I really have to give up everything again? Does it have to be like before?

And how long could she run? Where could she go that he wouldn't find her . . . again?

She shook her head, trying to think. The first thing she needed to do was to find out exactly what had happened, how he'd gotten out, how long he'd *been* out.

Reaching across the chair, she turned off the desk lamp, then started for the bedroom. If only her parents were back from Florida, she could call them and perhaps find out what she was suddenly desperate to know. They could contact the State Hospital, make an inquiry. But they wouldn't be back in Louisville for several days yet.

She entered the dark bedroom cautiously. Making her way to the night table, she wondered if she'd ever again be able to enter this room without her mind rerunning the image of that horrible doll.

She turned on the lamp, drawing in a shaky breath of relief when she saw the empty bed. She jumped when the light began to flash the signal for an incoming call.

Lifting the handset, she spoke, then waited.

It was Jennifer.

Devastated, Whitney watched the message about Daniel's . . . *accident* . . . float across the display.

She almost choked on her effort to respond to Jennifer's news. She was able to do no more than mumble a couple of brief questions, hoping her voice wouldn't betray the panic and fury boiling up in her.

When she finally replaced the receiver, she stood motionless, staring at the telephone for a long, tense moment.

Finally, she snapped off the lamp and flung herself across the bed with weak abandonment.

She lay without moving, helplessly angry, sick at heart, physically and emotionally drained. The details no longer mattered. Cory was out; he was here, and Daniel was his first victim.

After a long siege of hopeless weeping, she finally drifted into a restless sleep of savage dreams and silent cries for help.

12

The room was cold and in total darkness. Whitney forced her eyes open, rubbing them gently. They felt swollen from her bout of weeping and heavy with the beginning of a headache.

Something was wrong. She sensed it, lying there. Peering into the blackness, a cold wrapping of dread slowly settled over her. There was something different about the house.

For a long moment, she lay unmoving, trying to focus her eyes on some point of reference in the room. Finally, she turned her head, squinting in the direction of the digital clock on the bedside table. There was no display.

The power was off.

Was that what had awakened her, an awareness even while she slept that the house had been plunged into a frigid darkness?

She turned in the direction of the window across the room. Not a glimmer of light broke through.

Pushing herself the rest of the way up, she swung her feet over the bed and stood. The jacket to her dress was wadded around her waist, and she smoothed it down, pulling it tightly around her. Shivering from the cold and from a growing wave of unease, she felt for the brass knob at the foot of the bedstead. She gripped it, weaved slightly, paused for a moment to get her bearings. Then, extending her hand palm outward, she began to creep cautiously across the floor toward the window.

She felt her feet leave the braided rug and meet the

hardwood floor. Taking a few more steps, she stopped short, uttering a soft cry of pain when she stubbed her toe on the rocking chair in front of the window. She found the chair arm and skimmed her fingers over it, upward to the high wooden back. Moving around the chair, she put a hand to the drape and pulled it aside just enough to allow a narrow view.

It was as dark outside as in. No streetlights, no glow from the side porch light . . . nothing. Only a thick blackness that seemed to have swallowed the entire street. She could tell from the splattered window and sweeping shadows that the rain was blowing again.

Her hand clutched the drape, then let it slide through her fingers as she turned back to face the inky depths of the bedroom.

Now she was not only deaf, but for all practical purposes, blind as well.

This is what Daniel's world is like, she suddenly realized. Dark and shapeless with the continual threat of the unknown.

Her grogginess fled as panic seized her, threatening to suck her into a whirlpool of churning, hammering terror. Her senses distorted by fear, she felt as if something had taken hold of her, something . . . evil and cold and deadly. Instinctively, she struck out with both hands, slicing the air in front of her with a wild, defensive thrashing.

Abruptly, she stopped. *He had come for her . . . he was in the room, waiting for her to make a move, to try to run, to get away . . . .*

She edged sideways, away from the window, pressing her back to the cold wall.

Could he see her?

No, he wasn't in the room. He would have made his move by now, done something to torment her, terrify her.

But he could easily be in the house.

A flashlight. Where had she put her flashlight? She had

109

two: one in the office and another in the kitchen. At least she thought it was still in the kitchen. When had she last seen it? Where?

The cabinet under the sink.

She felt a sudden, desperate need for light. Another moment in this darkness would surely take her sanity. But what if he *were* in the room, waiting?

She made her decision. Lowering herself to her hands and knees, she began to crawl, slowly, carefully, through the clammy darkness.

The floor was hard and cold beneath her hands. Hysteria teased at the back of her mind. Her stomach suddenly pitched with the first throes of nausea.

She went on, feeling her way along the baseboard, desperately hoping that her movements were soundless. She felt like a terrified, caged animal trying to fight its way to freedom.

Oh, my Lord . . . cover me with your power . . . shield me, Lord . . . protect me, Father . . .

She was at the door to the hall. Scrambling through the opening on her knees, she paused to catch a breath, then got to her feet.

The hallway was as black as the bedroom. Hugging the wall, holding her breath, she began to move, expecting at any moment to be grabbed or struck.

Hesitating, she put both hands out in front of her, then flew across the hall into the kitchen.

Inside the room, she gasped for air and waited. When nothing happened, she moved forward, around the table, then to the sink.

Leaning one hand on the countertop, she pulled outward on one of the double doors beneath the sink. It came part of the way open, then stopped, shuddering on its hinge.

Tears of frustration stung Whitney's eyes as she dropped to the floor, pulling at the door with both hands, trying

110

desperately to be as quiet as possible. Finally, the handle gave, and the door shot open, almost knocking her off balance.

She grabbed the edge of the door. Thrusting her head forward, she began to feel among the cleanser and detergent bottles inside the cabinet, trying not to knock any of them over. She swept the right side, then the left.

The flashlight wasn't there.

She could no longer stop the tears. She wiped her cheeks with the back of her hand, trying to decide what to do next.

The closet in the office.

She remembered now. *Both* flashlights were in the office.

She had gone upstairs one day last week, late in the afternoon, to get a box of envelopes out of the storage room. The day had been gloomy, and, uneasy about encountering a mouse among the dusty cartons and crates stored in the unused rooms, she had gone to the kitchen to get the large flashlight. Before she started down the steps with the envelopes, she had tossed the flashlight inside the box to free both hands. Back inside the office, she had pushed the box into the closet—with the flashlight still inside it.

She nearly wailed with frustration. The office was at the other end of the house. She would have to go all the way down the hall in the dark, and—

And it was locked.

She would need the key from inside her purse. And the purse was still on the desk in the entrance hall.

She dragged in a long, shaky breath, trying to think.

All right . . . I'll go through the breakfast nook, back through the living room to the hall. I'll get the key from my purse, go back to the office . . . maybe by then the lights will be on.

She got to her feet, standing immobile for a moment, using the countertop to steady her shaking legs. Then she started to move, making her way out of the kitchen.

The pantry-sized breakfast nook seemed enormous as Whitney moved through it. She swallowed once, then again, against the wad of fear that seemed to be wedged in her throat. Reaching the wide, open archway into the living room, she stopped.

Candles.

She slapped a hand alongside her head, appalled at her own stupidity. There was a candle in almost every room of the house.

Matches . . . she had matches. On the mantle above the fireplace.

She started into the living room, moved too sharply and jabbed her elbow against the wall. Wincing, she kept moving until she came to the fireplace. She slid her hand along the smooth surface of the mantle top, from one end to the other.

The matches weren't there.

Frantic, she started at the other side and tried again. When she still couldn't find them, she got down on her knees and rubbed her hands along the hearth.

Finally, she stopped. For a long moment, she stayed that way, her empty hands splayed out in front of her, her head drooping between her arms.

Eventually, she lifted her head, staring numbly into the black void of the room. *Get up . . . get the key.*

She hauled herself to her feet, found the wall, and began to follow it, shivering at the touch of cold plaster. For the house to be this cold, the furnace must have been off for hours.

The power could be out because of the storm . . . it might not be what I'm thinking . . . . Power might be out all over town, for all I know.

She moved around the corner, into the entrance hall, feeling for the desk. Her hand hit the side of the lamp, and she felt it weave at the blow. Choking, she grabbed it, steadied it, waited.

After a moment, she went on fumbling for the purse, sliding her hand all the way across the desk. *It has to be here, I left it here.*

She dropped to the floor. Maybe she had knocked it off when she hit the lamp.

It wasn't there.

She scrambled to her feet, her mind racing. Without the purse, she had no keys. She couldn't get inside the office, couldn't get to the flashlight.

She was trapped in the darkness.

Call Michael. Hadn't he told her to, night or day? He'd given her his number, told her to memorize it—

But she *hadn't* memorized it. She had stuffed it in her purse, looking at it a couple of times afterward without really trying to commit it to memory. At that time, she wouldn't have considered calling him for help, a strange man . . . .

Leave the house . . . get out.

No . . . that might be exactly what he *wanted* her to do . . . he might be waiting outside, waiting until she ran out into the darkness . . . .

Unwillingly, Whitney forced her thoughts back, trying to remember how his mind worked. What *would* he expect her to do?

Run . . . he would be waiting for her to run.

He had loved to terrorize her, to wait for her in out-of-the-way places and jump at her when she least expected it. He would play one of his sick practical jokes—cruel stunts that grew more and more sadistic with time—then wait for her to react. Sometimes he would still be wearing his makeup from the players group, and he'd throw himself in her way, making those awful faces, then laughing at her . . . always laughing at her.

Hide . . . she would find a place to hide and stay there

113

until daylight.

A blow of urgency, a sweeping torrent of dread shook her, and she moved, stepping around the desk, feeling her way a few inches down the wall, to the closet door.

She opened the hall closet, pushed herself in, deep behind the out-of-season clothes she'd stored there. Gently pulling the door shut behind her, she edged all the way back to the rear of the closet, brushing aside the clothing that swiped her face as she moved. At the far corner, she sank down, pressing herself as tightly as possible against the wall. She settled herself, bending forward to hug her propped-up knees.

No longer trembling, she waited. Numb with cold, rigid with apprehension, she huddled in the corner, remembering. Remembering all the other times she had tried to hide from him.

She didn't know how long she stayed that way, crouched against the wall, praying for daybreak. Her legs ached; her shoulders felt stiff and swollen from trying not to move for so long a time.

Her awareness that something was happening dawned slowly, erratically. She sensed . . . what—movement?

She tensed, drawing herself even tighter against the closet wall. Her hands tightened almost painfully on her knees.

Light. At the bottom of the closet door, a silver strand of light weaved, disappeared, then returned. It stopped, held, then faded again.

He was there . . . outside the closet . . . .

She lifted a hand, balled it into a fist and stuffed it against her mouth to keep from screaming.

The light reappeared, wavered, grew brighter.

Without warning, the door exploded open. The beam of the flashlight shot through the closet, up, then to the floor. Clothes were jerked aside. The light scanned, dropped, found her.

114

Blinded as the white ball froze her in its glare, Whitney threw up her arms to shield her eyes.

She began to scream.

Abruptly, the light swept away from her face, and she felt hands grasping her shoulders, pulling her up to her feet, out of the corner, out of the closet.

The hands pried her arms away from her face, but she couldn't open her eyes ... *wouldn't* open her eyes ... she couldn't bear to see that face again ... she couldn't ....

But these hands were gentle. They smoothed back her hair, wiped the tears from her cheeks, pulled her close.

She opened her eyes.

"Michael?"

For a moment, she could do nothing but stare at him with blank incredulity. *But she hadn't called him ....*

It was his infinite gentleness that finally released her from the panic and coaxed her out of her dazed bewilderment. With the flashlight still burning, tucked under his arm, he put his other hand to her hair, stroking it, trying to soothe her. His eyes glistened in the indirect glow of the flashlight with a look that was both angry and anxious.

"Whitney ... *alannah* ... shh ... it's all right ... it's all right now. What's happened to you? I couldn't find you, I looked everywhere ...."

Half-sobbing, too weak with relief to answer him, Whitney dug her fingers into his jacket and clung to him.

He tried to draw her back, to look at her, but she only buried her face that much deeper into his shoulder.

He eased her a step away from the closet and propped the flashlight on the desk. Then he caught her shoulders with both hands and made her face him.

"Whitney, are you hurt?" His face was set, grim and worried.

She shook her head. "The lights went out."

He nodded, then prompted, "What happened?"

115

She looked at him. What *had* happened? She couldn't think . . . .

Putting one arm around her, Michael picked up the flashlight and steered her to the desk chair. "Here, sit down."

He watched her sink limply onto the chair. "Where can I find some matches and a candle?"

She shook her head. "There are candles . . . in almost every room. But I couldn't find matches."

He touched a hand to her arm. "I'll look. Stay here."

When he came back, he had a box of safety matches in one hand and a large, lighted candle in the other. "I found these in the kitchen," he said, pocketing the box and reaching for her hand to help her up. "Come on, let's move you to the couch; then I'll gather up some more candles." As she stood to her feet, Whitney glimpsed her purse, between the desk and closet door. She hadn't looked far enough.

Michael guided her into the living room, waiting until she sat down. Then he disappeared with the flashlight, returning after a moment with more candles. Soon he had at least a half dozen lighted candles spreading their soft glow through the room. He went to the fireplace, tossed on a couple of fresh logs, and built a fire. He waited until the flames were blazing high before coming to sit down beside her.

"Better?" he asked, settling himself on the cushion next to her and taking her hand.

She nodded, grateful for the warm strength of his hand enfolding hers.

He didn't try to make her talk, but simply sat in silence, watching her, occasionally giving her hand a reassuring squeeze. She remembered to look at her watch. It was almost five o'clock.

Still trembling, but beginning to pull herself back from the terror now, Whitney was finally able to speak. "Why . . . did you come?" A thought struck her, and she straightened, dropping his hand. "H-how did you get in?"

116

His gaze went to her hands, now clenched tightly in her lap. When he lifted his head, he studied her for a moment. "I came because of the lamp in the window."

At her frown, he explained. "I get up before dawn most days. It's the best time to work on my prints and get some of the writing done, so I can use the daylight hours for shooting."

Again he glanced at her hands, but made no move to touch her. "I realized something wasn't right when I woke up. I looked out and saw that the streetlight just across the way was off. Then I noticed the light in your office window wasn't on any longer. I decided to check." He paused, then added, "It would seem that the power is off all the way down the block, just on this side. Somebody vandalized a transformer, the electric company says. I called them to inquire."

She glanced across the room, to the entryway and the outside door. "How did you get in?" She watched his face intently.

He hesitated a moment, then told her, "I knew your doorbell wouldn't activate the signal light since the power was off. So I, ah, I'm afraid I took advantage of those office locks I was complaining about the other day. The credit card bit, you know." He gave her a cryptic smile, adding, "I did tell you they were worthless. Perhaps now you'll get them replaced."

She looked away, suddenly embarrassed by the memory of how he'd found her, huddled in the closet like a frightened child. And the way she had screamed when he opened the door . . . .

A gentle hand cupped her chin and turned her toward him. "Whitney . . . it's all right now. No one's in the house—I was all the way through it before I finally found you."

Feeling her face burn, she hoped the candlelight was too dim to betray her humiliated flush.

His features softened even more, and when he again

117

reached for her hand, she gave it willingly. "It must be an incredibly terrifying feeling . . . not being able to hear . . . or to see. I'm sorry that happened to you."

He understood. "I thought it was—"

Michael nodded, not letting her finish. "You thought someone was in the house."

Whitney hadn't the slightest doubt that someone *had* been in the house. She had felt his presence, sensed the corruption of his madness.

He dipped his head slightly, watching her. "Are you all right, *alannah*?"

Whitney frowned in puzzlement, repeating the unfamiliar word. "*Alannah*?"

He blinked, then smiled as his eyes went over her face. "It's the same as saying, ah . . . '*little one*'." After a moment, he added, "It's a Gaelic—endearment."

Their gazes met and held for a long time. His smile turned almost regretful when he finally spoke. "Let me take you to Jennifer's. You need to get some sleep, and you mustn't be alone."

The memory of Jennifer's telephone message hit Whitney full force. She sat up straighter, reaching out to clutch his arm. "You don't know . . . about Daniel, what happened—"

Quickly he drew both her hands together and enfolded them between his. "I do know."

At her frown, he explained, "I called their house after I left here tonight. I was thinking that perhaps I could drive out to the camp—ah, what's it called—"

"Helping Hand?" she supplied.

"That's it, yes. It sounded like an interesting place to shoot, perhaps do something on it in conjunction with the Friend-to-Friend Association. Actually, I was hoping you'd go with me, if Daniel were willing. Jennifer took my call and told me what had happened."

"Then you know *how* it happened?"

Nodding, he hesitated, then said, "And I know you're blaming yourself. Aren't you?"

Unnerved by his perception, Whitney didn't answer.

His hands tightened on hers. "Don't, Whitney. You're not responsible."

There was kindness in his eyes. But kindness didn't help. If only he knew . . . .

Bringing his face closer to hers to get her attention, he said, "You're exhausted. Get a coat and I'll take you to the Kaines so you can rest. You can't stay here."

She shook her head, pulling her hands away.

"Whitney—"

Her eyes started to fill, but she wouldn't weep. She wouldn't. She had to hold together. "Don't . . . please. I can't go up there. Not tonight." She would have to stay away from now on, of course. No matter how much she cared about them . . . *because* she cared about them.

Without touching her, he held her with his eyes. "You're sure?"

Nodding, she looked away. Jennifer would never understand, never stop trying. *Oh, Father, how can I hurt her like that? She's the best friend I've ever had . . . but I can't tell her the truth . . . I can't!*

When she turned back to him, Michael had left the couch and gone to stoke the fire. She watched him, kneeling on the hearth, his back to her. All his movements were so sure, so capable. What did he think of her? That she was emotionally unstable? Ill? How pathetic she must appear to him, a man who had probably never doubted himself in his life. Was it pity she had seen in his eyes tonight? The thought hit her hard, sickening her.

He returned, again dropping down beside her, closer this time. "All right, then, if you won't be moved," he said, watching her steadily, "the two of us will share a sunrise." He glanced down at his watch. "And soon, at that."

119

He leaned back, drawing her inside the shelter of his arm while settling her head gently against his shoulder.

Whitney hesitated for only a moment before letting herself relax against his strength, trying not to think about anything else except that he was going to stay with her until the darkness had passed.

In some way she couldn't begin to understand, he seemed to know instinctively that, at least for now, she needed nothing quite so much as she needed a friend. Obviously, he was offering to be that friend.

Whitney needed him too much to turn him away.

He reached a hand to cup her chin, turning her face to his so she could read his lips. His eyes were kind but determined. "Tell me about it, *alannah*. It's too big for you to go on carrying alone. Talk to me."

13

She was still talking when the first pale light of dawn cautiously threaded its way around the drapes and through the window.

The agony and torment she would have expected to feel at the replaying of that year of her life hadn't come. Instead, there had been an unexpected feeling of catharsis, an easing of the pain. She wondered if it would have been this way if her audience had been anyone but Michael.

She had thought that if the day ever came when she found herself able to talk about that awful, nightmarish time, it would be an event of excruciating emotion, a thundering experience that would take her back to the edge of terror.

Instead, it had been a quiet hour in front of a fire, with flickering candles and a man she scarcely knew who held her captive with his eyes. Rather than turmoil, she felt a growing calm, a sense of relief that she wouldn't have believed possible.

Michael had simply sat there, listening quietly, holding her hand through the entire story, watching her, prompting her, supporting her.

If his face had seemed grim and taut as she spoke, there was at least no condemnation, no apparent contempt for the naivete revealed by her tale. He seemed to understand and accept how a far more gullible Whitney could have become infatuated with a Louisville health club instructor.

She had met him when she enrolled in a self-defense course at the health club where she was a member. Cory

121

Ross was the instructor. He was new in town, had been in Louisville only two months. After the first class, he'd asked her for a date. She had refused, but he kept asking until, finally, she had given in.

Their first date had been a church praise festival. He'd said he was a Christian. She had believed him at first. She hadn't known, then, that he was brilliantly deceitful—or hopelessly insane.

"You said he was an actor," Michael was asking. "What kind of an actor?"

"Amateur groups," she explained. "Community theater, that type of thing. He was just getting involved in one of the local players groups when we met. He said it was only a hobby, an 'enrichment' experience. But it was more. He took it seriously. Far more seriously than he would ever admit."

Whitney wondered at the flinty edge in Michael's expression when he nodded, asking, "What attracted you to him in the first place?"

How many times had she asked herself that same question? Her answer came slowly, haltingly. "I don't know if you can understand this or not, but he appeared to be totally . . . normal. He looked like the boy next door. The captain of the football team. The son of your mother's best friend."

"Actually, that's a rather common sort of description for psychopaths," Michael said grimly. He seemed hesitant about his next question. His eyes searched her face closely when he asked it. "Were you in love with him?"

She looked at him, then glanced away. "No. Fascinated, maybe, but not in love. I'd never known anyone quite like him. He was clever. Intelligent. Unpredictable. Unconventional. And he'd only been in Louisville a couple of months. I suppose I was trying to be kind, at first."

His mouth thinned. "You'd do yourself an enormous

122

service, Whitney, if you'd learn to curb your missionary instincts a bit."

Anger flared, racing up through her so quickly she had to shut her eyes against lashing out at him. With a rigid effort, she kept it under control, saying nothing. He didn't understand, she reminded herself. Michael was a loner. She had already seen his confusion in the midst of a crowd, and he'd made no secret of the fact that his solitary life was a matter of choice.

He was the one who finally broke the silence. "After you realized he wasn't what he seemed, you tried to break it off?"

She nodded, instinctively hugging her arms tightly to her body. In spite of the fire blazing a few feet away, she felt cold. She moistened her lips, letting her gaze rest on the flames lapping at the logs in the fireplace. "He became intensely possessive. He seemed to be . . . obsessed with me, as if he didn't have any other life except for me. It reached the point that if he called my apartment and I didn't answer, he'd show up and stand in the hall, pounding on the door, shouting."

She took a deep breath, then went on. "Once I was there, inside the apartment, but when my signal light flashed and I saw him through the peephole, I didn't open the door. I was afraid to. I called Keith—my brother-in-law. He came right away and told Cory to leave." Swallowing hard as she remembered, she said, "He left. But not before he hit Keith hard enough to break his nose."

She lifted a hand and dragged it through her hair. Meeting his eyes for only an instant, she looked away. "I called him at the health club the next day, told him that if he didn't stop, I was going to the police. It didn't even faze him. He just laughed at me. He hadn't laid a hand on me, he said, so what could the police do?"

"All too true, unfortunately," Michael said, his mouth hard.

123

"I knew he had a temper," she went on, "but at first I didn't think too much of his threats. I thought he'd give up once he saw I wasn't going to be intimidated by him. I didn't return his calls, and I stopped going to the health club. I was hoping if I put enough distance between us, he'd just . . . forget about me."

She felt a tremor in her voice as she continued. "But he started harassing me continually after that. I'd come home and find my front door open, my dresser drawers emptied on the floor. Broken dishes in the kitchen, broken lamps . . . . "

A dark, chilling wisp of despair crept across her mind as she remembered. When Michael frowned and leaned closer, Whitney tried to force some strength into her voice so he could hear her better. "He knew that I had a horror of . . . spiders. And bees. I started to find them—dozens of them—in my kitchen cabinets, in the canisters . . . . "

Her words drifted off, and he made no attempt to prompt her. She felt herself skating backwards, fought it, clutching his hand as if to hold herself in the present.

He wrapped both of her hands inside his, watching her carefully.

" . . . I would come out of the school—I taught a night class for deaf adults then, in addition to the high school curriculum—and he'd be waiting for me. Around the corner of the building, in a dark place in the parking lot . . . he'd jump out at me and start to yell like some sort of wild thing. It made it worse . . . that I couldn't hear. He'd be dressed in one of the costumes from the players group. Sometimes he'd wear one of those . . . fright masks, the kind you buy at costume stores."

For a long moment, she sat unmoving, silently staring into the fire, aware that Michael's hands were now gripping hers even more tightly. When she turned to him, she tried to read the look in his eyes. Warmth, understanding—*and a glint of anger, too,* she thought.

124

"One night, after my adult class, he was in the parking lot, waiting for me. He was dressed in his own clothes, he seemed . . . calm. He begged me to go somewhere with him—to talk, he said. When I refused, he exploded."

Even now, remembering made her stiffen with fear. Cory's face had erupted into a storm of violent fury, the rage in his eyes like a blow. "He tried to force me into his car. When I fought him, it just made him crazier. He was like a-an animal. He threw me against the car, onto the ground . . . "

She couldn't finish for a moment. Michael said nothing, but simply held her hands, watching her. She squeezed her eyes shut for a few seconds, then opened them. Her voice was little more than a whisper when she spoke again. "He started beating on me . . . pounding at me with his fists . . . kicking me. All the time, he was screaming at me . . . I didn't know what he was yelling, I was too terrified to make it out."

She stopped, lifted her eyes to Michael. "He was strong. He worked out all the time, knew karate—" She felt her voice go to a whisper. "It *hurt.* I didn't know anything could hurt like that . . . my parents had never even spanked me when I was a child . . . I didn't know what it was like to be hurt that way."

Her pulse hammering, she realized that it was her own agony she saw burning out of his eyes. It was as if he were taking the blows with her, for her. He brought her hands to his mouth, brushed his lips over her knuckles as if he could somehow heal the ugly memories just by touching her.

" . . . I don't remember anything else," she went on, "not until I woke up in the hospital. Apparently, the night custodian had looked out and saw what was happening. He called the police, then ran outside to help me."

The sting of anguish in her eyes thickened to tears, and Michael tugged gently at her hands to pull her into his arms.

"Cory . . . almost killed Mr. Johnson—the custodian—

before the police got there. He beat him—he beat him almost to death." Her voice broke on a sob, and she clutched at his arm, trying to pull herself together.

When she had quieted, he pushed her just far enough away from him that she could read his lips. "They locked Ross up, then?"

Nodding, she blinked back the tears. "In the State Hospital for the criminally insane."

Searching her eyes, Michael said, "And now you think he's out?"

Her hands went to his shoulders, gripping hard. "I *know* he's out, Michael! I know it! He's here. Don't ask me how he did it. But he's *here!*"

He nodded, smoothing her tousled hair, wiping a smudge from her cheek with his thumb.

Calmer now, she said, "My parents have been in Florida, but they're due back in Louisville sometime next week. I'll have them check through the prosecutor's office to verify it, but I *know* he's not in that hospital anymore."

"The local police will be able to get more information on him than your parents could," he told her. "And we're going to talk with them first thing this morning. You have to give them all the details I couldn't." He paused, then said, "But Ross didn't escape."

"What?"

He shook his head. "He was released," he said with an expression of disgust. "Lots of conditions, of course. Twice-a-month counseling sessions, no drugs, no alcohol, no weapons, no out-of-state travel. The board felt that the, ah, patient had been rehabilitated and could now take his proper and meaningful place in the community. They ran a check yesterday. I had a call from one of the officers last night after I left you."

He was free. A free man. She almost laughed. Cory was free, and she was a prisoner.

126

A new thought struck her, and she asked, frowning, "Why are they being so helpful to you? Because you were a policeman?"

He shrugged. "The brotherhood and all that, I suppose."

Satisfied, she sighed and said, "I know you're right—that I have to talk with them. But do you think they'll still be willing to keep it quiet? At least for now?"

"I imagine they'll think it best if they do. It might give them an edge, not letting Ross know they're aware he's in the area. You're still worried about the Kaines, aren't you?"

"Yes. Surely you can understand why."

"I do, but I doubt that you'll be able to hold Jennifer off very long."

"I *have* to! After what happened to Daniel, I don't dare go near them until . . . "

Until what? She couldn't finish. She wasn't sure she really believed there would ever be an end to this. At least, not an end she could bear to think about. But even the thought of removing herself from Jennifer and Daniel's life twisted her heart. She loved them. And she thought they loved her. To give them up . . .

"You're finding this very difficult, aren't you?"

At her frown, he explained. "The idea of avoiding the Kaines? You care a great deal about them, don't you?"

"Yes," she answered weakly, looking at him. "You don't understand that, do you? My . . . needing them as I do."

His mouth tightened. "I don't, no. But I don't criticize you for it, either. It's your way, not mine."

From the beginning, she had found it impossible to believe that he was as hard, as independent as he seemed to believe himself to be. "Haven't you ever . . . needed anyone, Michael? Hasn't there ever been anyone . . . important to you?"

She saw him back off, saw the shutters click shut. He released her hands, then rose from the couch, turning away.

127

When he faced her again, his eyes were haunted, distant. "I had a sister," he said. "She's dead."

Stunned, Whitney got to her feet. She wanted to touch him, but his look rejected it.

"I'm sorry, Michael." Hesitating, she asked, "What happened?"

He looked at her for a long moment, and Whitney could sense the conflict going on inside him.

"We were orphans, actually," he finally replied. "Our parents died in a railway accident when we were small. Sile was only four at the time. After that it was a series of foster homes."

He glanced into the fire, then his gaze shifted to hers. "I was six years older than my sister, and when I came of age, I took custody of her. I did my best to give her a home, but it was—difficult."

He grew silent, as if he'd said far more than he'd intended.

"Difficult?" Whitney probed gently.

Again his mouth thinned. "I was just getting settled with the Constabulary. There was so little time to be with her, and she was still so young. She needed a real family—security, stability—all the things I couldn't seem to manage at the time. My own life was in chaos. I was just beginning to discover some of the—duties expected of me as a member of the RUC, and it was giving me real problems."

He shoved his hands deep into his pockets and glanced down at the floor for a time. When he again looked up, Whitney winced at the pain in his eyes.

"I was gone too much to know everything she was about. By the time I found out, it was too late. She'd gotten herself involved with one of the guerrilla groups. Sile was a born rebel, you see."

His face softened for an instant, and he even smiled a little. "She was always fighting for some cause or other, taking on

128

everyone else's battles for them. She was bright, brave, intense—all the lads were wild for her. She had such a sparkle about her. She could have done anything she set her mind to. Instead—" for the first time since he'd begun, he faltered, "—instead she ended up dead on the Falls Road. A bomb. It needn't have happened." It was said with unmistakable bitterness. "She ran out into the street to try and save one of her—friends. The bomb killed them both."

And she was all you had, Whitney thought. She moved to him, put her hand on his arm.

His eyes were fierce when he looked down at her. "She insisted on—thrusting herself into everyone else's life, on going to war for them." His eyes were shadowed, hollow with undisguised pain. "And it killed her."

"I'm sorry, Michael. She sounds . . . wonderful."

His face went cold. "Yes, wonderful. Wonderful, foolish, and dead."

No wonder he seemed so hard, she thought. His life had been hard. But his heart wasn't. She knew that. Even if he didn't.

"Is that when you left Belfast?"

He looked down at her hand on his arm, blinked, then released a long breath. "No. Not right then. It took me a bit longer to realize that I didn't want to spend the rest of my life as a hired gun pretending to be a policeman."

Placing his hands on her shoulders, he tried to smile. "We're very different, you and I. You've spent your life doing for other people, and I've spent mine avoiding them." He studied her face, searched her eyes.

"But you're a Christian. Daniel told me you are. How can you turn away from people and still be a Christian? That's a contradiction of the very meaning of the word, Michael."

The warmth in his gaze flickered out. "You think *God* doesn't turn away from His people?" he said bitterly.

He stared down at her, raw pain churning in his eyes. "Let me tell you something. I've seen God's people blown to bits in the middle of a Belfast street by bombs that weren't even meant for them. I've seen children gunned down in front of their own homes because their fathers didn't happen to believe the way the fellow behind the gun believed. I can tell you about entire families assassinated by a gang of teens who didn't have the faintest idea of the reason behind the killings."

He looked down at his hands on her shoulders, abruptly dropping them to his sides. "That's Ireland. But what about the States? What's different here? Street gangs rioting and violating. People killing children—child abuse, abortion. The homeless living in cardboard boxes in the depths of winter while churches spend their millions on amusement parks and limos and health spas."

His face twisted in a mask of resentment and angry defiance. "Where's God, Whitney? Tell me He hasn't turned away from His people. Go ahead—pick up your morning newspaper, and then tell me He still cares."

So much pain in him . . . so much anger, Oh, Michael, Michael, what would it take to heal your heart?

"It isn't God who's turned away," she said. "It's the rest of us." Exhausted, drained, and far too weak to even attempt a conversation like this, she said, simply, "I don't have any answers, Michael. Everything you said is true. I know what's happening. In Ireland, in America—everywhere, all over the world. And one person alone can't change it. But one person and then another person . . . and another . . . that can make a difference. It's Christ who makes the difference in us, so we can make a difference in the people around us. God hasn't turned away . . . Michael. It's just that we . . . can't see enough of the picture to understand what He's doing."

He stared down at her, again touching her hair. "You're a good little person, *alannah.* I only wish that particular trait weren't such a danger to you."

Letting his hand fall away, he crossed his arms over his chest and said, "I suppose you're going to insist on going to church this morning. Even though you haven't slept and you have no electricity."

When she nodded, he inclined his head in resignation. "Then we'll talk with the police afterward. I'll go along now if you're sure you'll be all right."

"Michael?"

He lifted a brow. His eyes were tired, she noticed, and he didn't look nearly as confident and self-contained as he usually did.

"You said you were going to be my shadow. Remember?"

He nodded, waiting.

"Does that mean you'll be at church, too?"

He gave her a look of grudging, but amused, respect. "I'll be there, lass," he answered. "Indeed, I'll be there."

14

Depression. By the following Tuesday, it was a word Jennifer had to face.

She sat at her desk late that morning, her office door closed, her studio monitor off, her heart heavy.

Turning away from the window, she rested her elbows on the desk, framing her face with the palms of both hands. What she couldn't quite grasp was how her life could have changed so much, so fast.

Without anger or censure, she honed in on the two people responsible for the change: her husband and her friend. Daniel and Whitney.

Whitney, of course, had been peculiar for days now. It was understandable that she'd be upset and skittish after that awful attack at the festival; Jennifer would have expected nothing less. But without question she had become even stranger since the arrival of Michael Devlin.

Whitney was avoiding her; that was clear, even if the reason wasn't. Although she'd been noticeably upset and genuinely concerned about Daniel's accident when she talked with Jennifer after the Sunday morning worship service, she had quickly—*too* quickly, Jennifer thought— declined an invitation to drop in later that afternoon.

That in itself wouldn't have made Jennifer think twice had it not been for the fact that the stone-faced Devlin had shown up at the church that morning, cornering Whitney after the service for what had appeared to be a very serious discussion. They had then walked outside together, his hand on Whitney's arm in a gesture that looked, Jennifer had

132

mused uneasily, almost possessive.

When Whitney hadn't so much as called the house or the station by Monday afternoon, Jennifer called her. It had been, she now thought dismally, an unsatisfying and unsettling conversation.

Her every attempt to coax Whitney to come by for a visit had met with evasion. Even when she pressed, commenting that Daniel "could use some cheering up," Whitney had still backed off from anything definite.

Later in the day, Lee Kelsey, one of the station's disc jockeys, innocently remarked that he'd seen Whitney and "that Irish guy" at Simpson's coffee shop the evening before. Jennifer had felt an instant of stinging rejection, hurt that Whitney could make time for the photojournalist but none for her friends.

When she complained to Daniel, his attitude left her feeling even worse.

"Jennifer, you're just not being objective about Whitney," he said shortly. "And you're being absolutely unfair to Devlin."

She'd been so sure he would understand her feelings that his unexpected disagreement made her miserable.

"Whitney's a normal, unattached young woman, and this man is single, new in town, and apparently interested in her." He spoke with forced patience, as if he were explaining something that should be easily discernible to a child. "Why *wouldn't* Whitney opt to spend an evening with him instead of coming up here to sit around with us and discuss my broken leg?" he'd added sourly.

Daniel, of course, was her *real* problem, she thought with a deep sigh as she buried her face even deeper inside her hands.

The alien and unexpected streak of brooding sullenness that had surfaced in her husband over the past few days had pitched Jennifer's world right off its axis.

133

She had never, *ever* seen Daniel pout. And even though the thought was difficult to accept, she was forced to admit to herself that Daniel was, indeed, *pouting*.

Up until yesterday, she had dismissed his general withdrawal and surliness as predictable. This morning, however, by the time she'd seen Jason onto the school bus and picked up most of the clutter from the previous day, she knew she could no longer ignore the morose fog in which Daniel had wrapped himself ever since the accident.

He had been sitting there, silent and lifelessly enthroned in his dilapidated old recliner, seemingly unaware of her presence in the room.

"Lee Kelsey is going to finish my afternoon drivetime for me so I can come home early today. I thought maybe you'd like to go for a ride later," she suggested hopefully.

"That's not even a possibility," he muttered after a moment. "There's no way I can get in and out of that Honda with—this." He flicked a hand over the top of his cast, managing a look of irritable distaste, even with his eyes closed. "And the Cherokee is too high."

"Oh. I didn't think of that." She decided to try another approach. "Well, I know what we *can* do," she said brightly. "Let's have your mother and dad over for dinner tonight. I'm in the mood for some company."

When he didn't answer right away, she prompted, "Daniel? Would you like that?"

After a deep, contolled sigh, he answered, "Jennifer, please stop trying to entertain me. It isn't necessary."

She bit her lower lip, shoved her hands into the pockets of her robe, and studied his face as dispassionately as possible.

"How do you feel, Daniel?"

He shrugged. "Okay."

"Is your leg bothering you?"

"No, it's fine." He stirred restlessly in the chair, as if trying

134

to maneuver himself into a comfortable position.

"You're not in any pain?"

He opened his eyes, and she thought she sensed a small flicker of impatience cross his features. However, he merely shook his head and replied quietly, "No. At least, not right now."

She hesitated. "Then what's wrong?"

"Wrong?"

"If you're not in any pain, and if your leg isn't bothering you, then what *is* bothering you?"

He drummed the fingers of his left hand on the chair arm. "Bothering me?"

"Don't do that! You know it irritates me."

He looked genuinely surprised. "Don't do what?"

"*That!* Don't answer my questions by asking your own. You always do that when you don't want to admit you know exactly what I mean."

"But I *don't* know what you mean," he said with maddening calm as he resumed the finger-thumping.

"Daniel, you have been a *stone* for days now, ever since you broke your leg! You don't talk to me; you don't even smile at me. I might as well be a—a *chair* for all the reaction I get from you!"

He straightened slightly, lifted his chin a fraction, and, much to her relief, stopped tapping his fingertips. "I'm sorry. I didn't realize."

Suddenly contrite, she said, "Oh, I'm sorry. I shouldn't have said anything. I know this is awful for you."

Quickly, he shook his head, waving away her attempted apology. "No, I'm sure I haven't been very good company."

"Daniel, I'm not expecting you to be good company. I'm just concerned because you don't usually—"

Pout. She had almost said it. Biting her lip even harder, she went to him. She squeezed his shoulder, then bent to kiss him on the forehead. "I just feel frustrated because I don't know how to help you."

His expression gentled, and he pulled her down beside him on the chair arm. "No, you're right. I've been rotten."

He sighed, shifted slightly in the chair, and said, "I feel like such a lump, Jennifer. Useless. You're doing everything for me—even more than usual, and I can't do anything about it except sit here, congealing in this chair. I can't walk, I can't swim—I can't do anything but make life more difficult for you."

"Daniel, you *know* I don't mind doing things for you!" she insisted, appalled at the direction of his thoughts.

Nodding, he again put his head back. "I know you don't. But *I* mind."

The thing was, she didn't do that much. He wouldn't let her. Still, he obviously felt helpless, as if he were being a burden.

Anger surged anew in Jennifer as she considered the extreme cruelty that had been inflicted upon her husband by someone who most likely would never know—or care about—the extent of the damage he had caused.

Again, she kissed him, this time on his bearded cheek. "Daniel," she said softly, "I *do* understand. I really do. I just wish there were something I could do to change things for you."

He had squeezed her hand and even managed a small smile, but said nothing more.

So now she sat glumly at her desk, her mind locked on the fact of her husband's depression—and her own. At the back of her thoughts, there was still the puzzle of Whitney's odd behavior, but she simply couldn't deal with that right now. First she had to think of something to help Daniel.

She glanced at her watch. It was almost time to set up for her afternoon show. Dragging in a long breath, she pushed herself up from her chair. As she walked into the studio, she

136

realized she hadn't yet called Daniel's mother about dinner tonight. Going to the console to check some settings, she waved at Lee in the opposite studio, then turned and went to the phone.

It occurred to her as she picked up the handset that perhaps she should attach a plea for help to her dinner invitation. Pauline Kaine was a wise, caring lady, and while Jennifer was fairly certain that Daniel's practical, sunny-natured mother would have no firsthand knowledge of the blues, she might at least have some insight or advice to offer.

Leaving word with the school secretary for Pauline to call her before her next class, she returned to the console, put on her headset, and waited for her cue.

She felt better already. As the light went on, she forced a smile into her voice over the lump in her throat and opened her mike.

"Hello, everybody. It's 12:30 in Shepherd Valley. This is Jennifer Kaine, and I've got some Good News for you . . . . "

Half-dozing, Daniel heard a key turn in the front door even before Sunny barked. He stirred and shook his head, groggily aware that he'd slept through the last part of Jennifer's show.

He listened to Sunny pad over to the front door, no longer barking, but now whining with excitement.

"Daniel? It's just me, dear." The door closed. "Yes, Sunny, I see you, too. Want your ears rubbed, do you?"

"Mom?" He sat up, wiped a hand over his eyes, then his chin. "What are you doing here?"

"School's out. It's almost 3:00."

He felt a rush of air as she breezed up to him and planted a kiss on top of his head. "I just thought I'd stop in and get the spaghetti sauce started for Jennifer. Jason's not home yet?"

Daniel breathed in her soft, familiar baby powder scent and again shook his head to wake up. "The bus doesn't come until almost 4:00." He yawned, saying, "If Jennifer talked you into making the sauce, that must mean you and Dad are coming to dinner."

"We are indeed. And I'm looking forward to it. This family has had precious little time together lately, it seems to me. As soon as your sister and Gabe get back, I'm going to have all of you over for lasagna."

"You won't have to ask twice."

He listened to her brisk steps cross the living room, the dining room, then enter the kitchen. The three rooms were undivided by walls, so Pauline talked to him as she worked.

"Jennifer still doesn't trust her sauce," she said distractedly, "though I don't understand why."

"I think she's just intimidated by yours." He smiled a little to himself. "With good reason."

"Jennifer's a very good cook, Daniel, and you shouldn't tease her about it."

Daniel stretched, then dropped his hands onto the arms of the chair, comparing the sounds she made in the kitchen to Jennifer's style. His mother even *sounded* efficient when she cooked, he thought. Whereas Jennifer usually banged and clanged and occasionally crashed, his mother clicked and hummed and whirred, singing softly as she worked.

He leaned back against the chair. The sounds coming from the kitchen were oddly comforting, and for a moment he felt almost guilty, as if he were somehow betraying Jennifer.

It's called regression, Kaine. It's a lot easier to reminisce about the good old days than to deal with the grim reality of the present.

"Daniel?" Apparently, his mother had asked him a question.

"Sorry, Mom. What?"

"I asked if you want me to make some coffee."

He nodded. "That sounds good."

When the coffee was done, she returned and set a tray on the table beside him. "Here we are. I found some cookies in the jar, too," she said, gently guiding his hand to the tray so he'd know where it was.

He heard her sit down on the couch across from him. "Thanks, Mom."

"Eat some cookies, too. You look a little thin, Daniel."

He couldn't stop a grin. "Mom, I've been a lump for four days now. My total physical activity has consisted of picking up a fork and opening my mouth. There's no possible way I could look thin."

"Still—"

"I'll eat the cookies."

In his mind he pictured her, his memory bringing her clearly to the screen of his thoughts. She would be perched forward, tall and trim, on the couch cushion, her hands clasped quietly in her lap. Her large, warm eyes—eyes that were a rich, uncommon shade of taupe—would be fastened on him with a combination of motherly concern and discomfiting sharpness.

"Jennifer's a wonderful girl, Daniel. Do you know how blessed you are?"

Surprised, he set his cup down. "Of course, I know. What brought that on?"

"You're depressed, aren't you, Daniel?" Her tone was sympathetic.

He groaned.

"What is it, dear? The pain?"

He expelled a long breath, suppressing his impatience. "No, I'm fine, Mom. Really."

"But you *are* depressed."

"No," he said defensively. "I know about depression. This

isn't depression."

"I see. What is it then, dear? What's wrong?"

"*Nothing's* wrong, Mom. What would you and Jennifer like me to do? Hop around and wave my crutch in the air to show how much I'm enjoying all this?"

His face grew hot in the silence. "I'm sorry," he said quietly. "That was uncalled for."

She was silent for a full half-minute, then said mildly, "It's all right. I understand. But you're right, Daniel. You're not depressed."

He took a sip of coffee, relieved at warding off a maternal lecture.

"You're feeling sorry for yourself."

He burned his throat on the coffee as it lodged, halfway down. Mother or not, he'd just about had the day's limit of women probing his emotional barometer. He wouldn't argue, of course. One of the first lessons Lucas Kaine had taught both his children was that neither of them, for any reason, were ever to argue with "my wife." In matters of discipline, Daniel remembered wryly, he and Lyss had always had a sure-fire way of measuring their father's seriousness: if he referred to their mother as "my wife," it was heavy stuff. A closed case.

"I know about feeling sorry for yourself, Daniel. I know exactly what you're feeling."

When he would have disputed her words, she stopped him. "You wouldn't remember—you were only a baby—a few months old. But you've heard your father and I talk about that awful time I had to spend in a sanitarium. When I had tuberculosis."

He had forgotten. Any reference to his mother's earlier illness had always been brief and quickly dismissed by his father, who candidly admitted he didn't like to think about it.

"There I was, a year out of college, a young wife, a new

140

mother with a baby son. And I had to leave everything—you, your father, our home—to go and stay in that awful hospital." She stopped, and there was a rare unsteadiness in her voice when she added, "I was terrified. Absolutely terrified."

He leaned forward, his interest captured. It was something he'd never really thought about. Neither parent ever gave the experience more than a passing word, an unpleasant frown of remembrance. For the first time he wondered what it had been like for her.

"How long did you have to stay there?"

"Months." She uttered a short, dry laugh. "It might just as well have been years. I *mourned*, Daniel. I actually mourned for you and your father, as if you were dead to me. I worried constantly about whether or not you'd even remember me when I came home. I worried about whether your father would still love me. I became almost obsessively frightened about our marriage. It was so painful, knowing I was missing your first words and your first steps—all those wonderful firsts that mean so much to a mother."

"Grandpa Dan and Grandma Lou took care of me, didn't they?"

"Yes, and I don't know what Lucas would have done without them. He was just setting up his practice when I got sick." Her voice was low and unsteady when she added, "It was a *terrible* time in our lives."

She sighed deeply, then went on. "The worst part of the entire ordeal, for me, was knowing that your grandmother was doing all the things *I* wanted to be doing. Not that I resented her for it—I loved her like my own mother—but I felt so *guilty*. There she was, trying to manage her own work and mine as well. I *hated* that! It made me feel so *useless*. And so helpless."

"You said the first few weeks," he prompted gently. "It got better after that?"

141

"It wouldn't have if your Grandpa Dan hadn't written me a very special letter."

Daniel could hear the faint smile of remembrance in her voice as she went on. "Your father had confided in him—poor man, he had to unload on *someone*. Anyway, your Grandpa Dan wrote me this wonderful letter that simply overflowed with love—and a whole storehouse of wisdom."

She stopped for a moment, and Daniel heard her rise from the couch and walk in the direction of the fireplace.

"He understood. He was a man who always had a keen sensitivity about the feelings of others, you remember that. He explained to me how it was with your grandmother: that taking care of you and Lucas wasn't a burden, but a blessing for her, that she was happiest when she was pouring herself out for others. He said that if it hadn't been you and Lucas who needed her, she would simply be spending herself on someone else. That was just her way, he said. Her nature."

He squirmed a little, beginning to sense her point.

"And that's your Jennifer's way, Daniel," she said quietly, coming back to put a hand on his shoulder. "Jennifer could no more feel burdened by doing things for you or Jason—or for anyone else—than she could stop loving you. The girl has so much love to give that she's always looking for new ways to give it."

His throat tightened as he felt her squeeze his shoulder. "It's just as your Grandpa Dan said, dear. People like your grandmother and Jennifer are those who make love an active verb. They have a servant's heart. It's as natural for them to do for others as breathing. What's difficult for the rest of us is to *receive*. We get so caught up in self-pity and pride—and our determination to be self-sufficient—that we don't see what we're doing, that we're actually rejecting their love. Sometimes, Daniel," she said thoughtfully, "you love best by accepting the love of others."

He felt a dawning recognition begin somewhere deep inside him. Nothing she had said was new. He'd heard it before, knew it in his heart. But it had always been so difficult for him to acknowledge his own weakness, even with his wife. And the fact was that he needed her—desperately. The rest of it was that Jennifer's love was his. His need—and her willingness—that's what he had to accept.

He covered his mother's hand on his shoulder with his own, and she bent to touch her cheek to his. "Daniel, let your wife love you. Right now, you need to take. And Jennifer needs to give. Don't throw her love back at her. Don't you see, dear, that the greatest hurt you can inflict on her is to reject what she's trying to offer? Don't do that to her, Daniel."

Not waiting for a reply, she gave him a hug, then kissed him once more on the forehead. "I have to run, dear. Your father and I want to stop at the nursing home and look in on Aunt Serena before we come over tonight."

"Mom—"

"Tell Jennifer the sauce is all done except for a little more oregano later. I left the heat—oh, here she comes now."

Daniel heard the key turn in the door and eagerly leaned forward at the sound of Jennifer's voice.

"I hope that wonderful smell coming out of my kitchen is what I think it is."

"It is, dear," Pauline answered, moving away from Daniel, "but if I don't get out of here, I'm not going to be back in time to enjoy the fruits of my labor."

Impatiently, he listened to the two women draw out their good-byes before the door closed and Jennifer finally came to graze his cheek with a slightly hesitant kiss.

He reached out a hand to her, drawing her down beside him on the chair arm. "I missed you."

Her voice was guarded when she answered. "Is something wrong, Daniel?"

143

"No, nothing's wrong," he said quietly. "Not now."

Sensing her confusion when she remained silent, he pulled her closer and wrapped her in his arms.

"Daniel, I might hurt your leg—"

"The leg's fine. Forget the leg." He lifted a heavy wave of hair and let it sift slowly through his fingers.

"Daniel, are you sure everything is all right—"

"Everything is very much all right." He kissed her. Soundly.

Afterward, she pulled in a long, shaky breath. "I'm glad you're feeling better, darling."

He laughed. "I've been that bad, huh?"

"That bad?" she repeated warily.

"Mm. Listen, I need your help. If you don't mind," he added soberly.

"You do?"

Smiling at the pleased note he heard in her tone, he nodded. "I know you'll be busy tonight, with the folks coming over and all. But I thought maybe tomorrow morning, before you go in to the station, you might help me get set up at the piano instead of in this chair. I've got the music for a new song going through my head," he explained, "and I'd like to work on it for awhile."

She hugged him tightly around the neck, and he could hear the relief in her voice. "Oh, I'm *glad*, Daniel! Of course, I'll help you. I'd *love* to help you!"

"I thought you would," he said softly, gratefully burying his face in the sweet silk of her hair.

"What kind of a song is it, Daniel?"

He smiled. "I'm pretty sure it's going to be a love song, darlin'."

15

By 8:30 Wednesday morning, Whitney had five people in her office. Two wheelchair-bound members of Friend-to-Friend; their two drivers—teenagers from the local Christian high school who served as volunteers under a work-study project; and Stephanie Lowe, a county social worker who needed Whitney's testimony in an upcoming hearing on an abuse case involving a handicapped child.

She also had a leak in the office. Something had given way in the ancient, unused bathroom upstairs, causing a narrow but persistent stream of water to break through the ceiling only a few feet away from the desk. So far, she'd managed to control it with buckets and a plastic shower liner; she continued to hope for a free moment to call the plumber.

Added to this was a phone that had been jammed for over thirty minutes with messages scurrying across the display, each demanding immediate attention.

Given the fact that she hadn't slept for two nights, Whitney sensed an impending disaster. It seemed that the entire day was already out of control.

Her emotions took the riot a step further when Michael walked in unexpectedly.

Whitney was bent over her desk signing travel expense checks for the drivers when the door opened. She looked up, watching as his expression went from curiosity to amused incredulity.

His gaze shifted from the drivers to the impatiently tapping foot of the case worker, then locked on the plastic runner with buckets lined up like a small brigade of galvanized guards.

Glancing upward from the buckets to the stained ceiling, he finally turned his attention on Whitney. "This, ah, might not be the best time to talk with you?"

Straightening, she lifted a hand to indicate that he should wait, then gave each of the drivers a check. With a smile, she fended off the mischievous Jonathan Kaylor's weekly attempt to flirt with her as he wheeled his chair down the ramp.

Behind Kaylor was Becky Price. A cerebral palsy victim confined to a wheelchair for most of her 25 years, Becky had a smile people remembered for hours and a warmth even the coldest of hearts couldn't resist.

Whitney gave her a quick hug before closing the door and turning to the fiery-haired case worker, already on her feet and headed toward the desk.

"Whitney, here are the notes you said you wanted for the hearing Friday," she said, her words spilling out in a rush as she stared at Whitney over the rim of her glasses. "I tried to give you an idea of what type of questions to expect, but be prepared for anything. We're dealing with a defense attorney who's a crazy man and a prosecutor whose metabolism runs on leaded fuel only." She looked down at the file in her hands and shrugged.

"Stephanie . . . slow down, please," Whitney interrupted.

The case worker glanced up. "What? Oh, sorry, your eyes can't keep up with my mouth, huh? Understandable. What's wrong, Whitney?" she asked, peering sharply over her glasses. "You look tired."

Reaching for the file, Whitney smiled at her. "I'm fine. Things have been . . . hectic."

Stephanie nodded, thrusting the file at Whitney. "I know hectic. Listen, I have to run. I've got an adoption hearing at nine."

"Wait a minute," Whitney said, picking up a small piece of memo paper. "I had a message on my machine yesterday. It came in while I was at lunch—apparently from someone at the Social Services Office." Whitney handed her the note. "They want me to make a call on this man today. Do you know anything about it? The message said it's urgent."

The social worker glanced at the note. Shaking her head, she handed the message back to Whitney. "I don't know who called, but you'll probably be wasting your time. We've had a couple of investigators out there over the past year, and they got zilch from him. From everything I've heard, old Tom Power is a dedicated hermit. What are they wanting you to do, sweet-talk him into accepting some help? They're probably worried he's starving to death up there on top of his mountain." Without giving Whitney time to respond, she asked, "Are you going?"

"I suppose so," Whitney answered uncertainly. "I can at least try."

"Brave girl. Let me know if you get anywhere."

When the signal for the telephone flashed, Stephanie backed off with a quick wave. "I'll get out of your hair. Thanks, Whitney. I'll call you." Brushing Michael's arm on the way out, she charged out of the office at a run.

Whitney started to answer the phone, shooting a harried smile of apology in Michael's direction. He grinned at her and walked the rest of the way into the room. "Go ahead," he told her, gesturing toward the phone as he perched on the side of her desk to wait.

The display lighted as soon as she lifted the handset and said hello.

"Whitney, it's Jennifer."

Caught off guard for a moment, Whitney stared blankly down at the display. Then, recovering, she answered, giving Michael an anxious look as she said, "How are you, Jennifer? And Daniel—how's he feeling?" She sank down onto the

147

chair behind her desk.

"Daniel's doing fine, but I could use a friend." There was a pause. *"Where have you been?"*

"I—I knew you'd be . . . busy," Whitney stammered inanely, "with Daniel's accident and all."

"I've missed you, Whitney. Listen, Daniel and I were wondering if you'd come to dinner Saturday night? Jason's begging to see you."

Her eyes still on Michael, Whitney fumbled for an answer. "Saturday night? Well, I . . . "

"We thought you might like to ask Michael Devlin to come, too."

Startled, Whitney looked at him. "Michael? Well, I . . . could ask him, of course, but I don't know—"

His brows shot up in a questioning look of surprise, and he bent over her desk to watch the display with her.

"Good. We'd love to have you both. Are you having a busy day? I thought maybe you could stop by the station later and we'd go to lunch."

She was tempted. She missed their lunches, their talks . . . their friendship. "I'm sorry, Jennifer, I can't today. I have to drive out to—" she glanced down at the note still in her hand—"Blackwater Run early this afternoon."

Michael's hand covered hers as he gave her a look that clearly said he knew her response had caused her pain.

There was a pause, then, *"Blackwater Run? That's almost ten miles out, Whitney—and straight up the side of a mountain. Why are you going up there?"*

Whitney explained about Thomas Power and the request for a contact.

Jennifer's response was immediate. *"Do you know how to get there?"*

"Vaguely. I know it's close to the Campground."

"That's right. Remember the flea market we went to a couple of weeks ago, at Gage Park? Just drive out to the

148

Park, but instead of turning left at the gate, turn right at Fannon Lumber. That's Holly Hill; Blackwater runs off it, about two miles straight up. You'll see a sign." Another pause, then, "Are you going out there alone?"

Whitney was unable to stop a smile. Even over an LCD display, Jennifer's protective instincts came through. "Yes, Jennifer."

Her eyes widened when Michael gave her a look and shook his head, mouthing, "No, you're not."

"Whitney, Tom Power has an awful reputation. Everybody says he's a stubborn, cantankerous, grouchy old man."

"Sounds as if he'll fit right in with the rest of my day," Whitney said with a sigh. "Relax, Jennifer. I've encountered crusty old men before."

"I wish I didn't have to jock the afternoon show, I'd ride out there with you."

Whitney interrupted her. "I'll just threaten to send you out next time if he gives me any trouble. Jennifer, I really have to go—it's a circus here this morning."

After an instant, Jennifer's reply came back. "Okay. You won't forget about Saturday night?"

"I'll . . . call you back on it, all right?"

After hanging up, she looked at Michael. His hand was still on hers, and he was studying her face with a look that made her feel . . . what? It made her feel *good*, she decided tenuously. Special. It made her feel like nothing else had ever made her feel before.

Dipping his head a little closer, he said, "Please tell me this is not a routine morning in your life. I'd hate to believe that you start every day like this."

Caught for a moment in the magnetic field of his eyes, she reluctantly eased her hand away from his, dragging it through her hair. His eyes followed the movement, then returned to her face.

149

"No," she replied with a weak laugh. "Sometimes it's worse."

Still leaning close, his gaze unwavering, he asked, "And you didn't sleep last night either, did you?"

"I—"

He wagged a finger at her. "Don't ever try to lie, Whitney. Not with those eyes."

She smiled sheepishly. "Jennifer asked us to dinner," she told him, trying to divert his attention.

Easing himself off the desk, he glanced down at the phone. "You're certain that wasn't a hacker breaking into your call?"

When she didn't answer, he put a hand on her shoulder.

She looked up.

"I'd love to have dinner at the Kaines. With you." He squeezed her shoulder.

"But—"

"This is a way you can spend some time with them and not worry about the consequences. Tell her we'll come."

"It still involves them."

"Whitney—" he dropped down to a stoop beside her chair. "Trust me."

She met his gaze and said, simply, "I *do* trust you. But you can't stop him."

"You obviously don't know the reputation of the RUC."

"What?"

He released her shoulder and got up, again perching on the edge of the desk. "There have been some very pointed charges made about Northern Ireland's finest," he explained with a grim smile. "Suffice it to say that they're a rough bunch of lads, the occasion calling for it."

"I read the papers, Michael."

His eyes left her face. "Then you must know that I'm most likely not a very nice man."

She put a hand to his arm, and he looked back to her. "I don't know what you used to be," she said softly. "And I don't think I care. But I know you know the Lord, and it seems to me that you *are* a very nice man."

His gaze scanned her face for a long moment. Finally, he broke the mood by saying, "If you're to go on thinking I'm a good fellow, I'd best take a look at your plumbing problem." He motioned to the brown stain on the ceiling which was still releasing a steady stream of water.

She sighed. "It's probably a broken pipe."

He stood up. "I'll have a look. Perhaps I can patch it until you get someone in. It'll keep me out of your way until lunch time."

"Lunch time?"

"Yes, I thought we'd have lunch before facing the bear in his den."

"Michael—"

"Actually, it will give me a chance to shoot some landscape," he said, ignoring her attempted protest. "We'll take the Bronco. My equipment takes up a good deal of space."

"Michael, it's several miles out—"

"More the better. I'm itching to get at these mountains. They're glorious." Resting his hands lightly on her shoulders, he grinned down at her. "Don't ever, ever argue with an Irishman, Whitney. We invented the art. Come on, now, be a good lass and show me how to get upstairs."

Smiling, she led him out into the hallway, stopping by the dark, narrow door that opened onto the stairs. "I hate it up there," she said, wrinkling her nose as she flipped the light switch.

At his puzzled glance, she explained. "Mice," she said meaningfully.

"Ah, yes." He nodded with understanding, then tapped his inside left shoulder, saying, "Not to worry."

151

She frowned at him in puzzlement.

He stared down at her with a measuring expression, then slowly parted his jacket to reveal a shoulder holster.

Whitney felt as if her entire body had suddenly been whisked inside an icy sheet. Her eyes went from the gun to his face.

"That was a mistake," he said tightly. "You don't like knowing about this, do you?" He closed his jacket.

"Why do you still carry a gun?" she asked quietly. "You're not a policeman anymore."

He looked at her, then touched the palm of his hand gently to her cheek. "But the bad guys are still out there, aren't they, *alannah*?"

Turning away from her, he started up the stairs.

As Jennifer hung up the phone with a sigh, Daniel asked, "So—how'd it go?"

She turned to look at him. He was already at the piano this morning, propped comfortably in an enormous barrel-back chair with a stool shoved in front of him to elevate his leg. His computer was running a music-composing program on a table at his left; a pot of fresh coffee sat on a stand at his right.

"She didn't say no."

"Did you tell her to ask Dev, too?"

"Oh, yes," she replied grudgingly. "That's when she seemed to warm up to the idea."

"Hm. Maybe they *are* working on something serious here."

"She couldn't make lunch, though," she said worriedly.

"Did she say why?"

"Yes, and I'm a little apprehensive about her reason, Daniel," she said, walking over to the piano. "She's driving up to Blackwater Run this afternoon. To see Thomas Power."

He frowned. "Who's responsible for that?"

"She didn't say, just that she'd had an urgent request from someone at Social Services." She paused. "I don't like the idea of her going way out there by herself. That's a terrible road out to Holly Hill, and it gets even worse going up the mountain." She balled a fist under her chin and added, "Not to mention what kind of a reception she's likely to get from that—hermit."

"Tom Power's not a hermit," he said mildly, giving the keyboard another couple of strokes and wincing at the weird sound that greeted his effort. "Wrong mode," he mumbled. "He's just a lonely, crippled old man who took a beating for half a century in the coal mines. Never married, never let anyone get close to him. No friends that I've ever heard about. He's had enough to make a man a little cranky."

"You know him?"

He chuckled and shifted his weight in the chair. "He ran Gabe and me off his mountain a couple of times when we were teenagers, yeah. He was one mean rascal back then."

"Well, from what I've heard he hasn't mellowed any. I certainly hope he doesn't take his temper out on Whitney."

Again he laughed softly. "You underestimate your little buddy. She could turn back a swarm of mad bees if she set her head to it. Whitney's a lot sturdier than you think she is."

"I hope you're right." She watched him make a face at the next distorted cadence that marched out of the speaker. "Whatever happened to that love song you were going to write?"

"I'm working on it," he answered testily.

"Define *love*."

His hand stopped, suspended above the keyboard, as he raised his head and sighed patiently.

"Kiss me good-bye, Jennifer."

"You want anything before I leave, Daniel?"

He nodded and went back to his keyboard. "How about a little respect?"

16

The Bronco lived up to its name, bucking to a stop after the roughest ride Whitney had ever experienced. As she closed her eyes and waited for her stomach to break free from her throat, she silently promised herself that she would never ride a mountain road with Michael Devlin again.

Taking a close, somewhat apprehensive look at Thomas Power's residence, she couldn't help but wonder if the ride might not turn out to be the best part of the afternoon.

The place gave every appearance of being, in Michael's words, a "hermit's lair." Isolated against a densely wooded hillside, the small, unpainted cabin with its dusty windows and grim appearance seemed to shout a warning that visitors would not be welcome here.

As they got out of the car and approached the porch, however, she took heart from the splash of fall flowers blooming all across the front of the cabin. Someone had gone to the trouble of adding some beauty and color to the otherwise dingy little home; she took that as a sign that the owner might not be as intimidating as she'd heard.

Her hopes were dashed when three minutes of vigorous knocking produced no response.

She tried to call out as she knocked, but Michael gently gestured to her with a shake of his head and a finger over her lips that her voice was too soft to be heard inside. He took over, pounding with a large fist while calling out Power's name.

When the door unexpectedly flew open, Whitney flinched and took a step backward, prepared for the worst. Standing straight, his shoulders braced in readiness, Michael watched the doorway with a look of frank curiosity.

The stooped, glowering man who appeared at the door wasn't what Whitney had expected. Not a big man, his height was dwarfed even more by the slightly bent posture required to lean heavily upon a walker.

Whitney's first sensation was one of genuine sympathy. *The poor, gray man,* she thought, smiling at him while he glared first at her, then at Michael. From head to toe, Thomas Power was colorless. His silver hair, looking uncombed but clean, topped an almost ashen face. Even the eyeglasses resting on his hawklike nose were rimmed with silver, the eyes behind them as cold as gun metal. A worn charcoal cardigan hung open across a gray work shirt and darker gray pants.

Power lifted his chin, so narrow and pointed it almost appeared to curl upward in an angry, stubborn crescent.

Unabashed by the man's obvious hostility, Whitney nevertheless recognized the need to tread carefully. "Mr. Power? I'm ... Whitney Sharyn. From the Friend-to-Friend Association." Glancing at Michael, she went on. "And this is Michael Devlin. We'd like to visit with you for a few minutes if it's convenient."

Pinning her in place with a belligerent, steely-eyed glare, Power gave no indication he had heard her.

It occurred to Whitney that she really wasn't up to this, but she stood her ground, meeting the elderly man's stare with a level look of her own. "Could we come in, Mr. Power?"

He surprised her by snapping, "Why?"

Whitney looked at him blankly, fumbling for the right words. "Are you familiar with the ... Friend-to-Friend Association, Mr. Power?"

He straightened an inch or so upward, and Whitney saw that his hands on the walker were white-knuckled, as if the slight movement had caused him intense pain. "No, I am not," he snarled with a menacing look. "Nor do I want to be."

Studying him, Whitney saw a man who was probably in his mid-seventies, a man severely crippled by arthritis and possibly a mine accident as well. His right leg was bent in toward the left at a forty-five degree angle, as if it hadn't been straight for years. When he shifted on the walker, his arms appeared to be rigid and unbending. He was, she decided, a man who could use a helping hand, even if he resisted the idea. And she had little doubt that he *would* resist it.

Caution giving way to compassion, she met his gaze with a steady look. "I'd like to talk with you, Mr. Power. I think Friend-to-Friend could be of some . . . help to you, if you'll just let me come in and explain—"

Her words seemed to stoke a blaze of resentment in him. His face contorted into an expression of pure nastiness as he lashed out at her. "I don't need your help! I don't want your help!" With the obvious intention of slamming the door in their faces, he started to turn away.

Whitney was unaware that Michael, beside her, had spoken until she saw Thomas Power turn back and shoot the photographer an angry, suspicious look.

Glancing up at Michael to read his lips, she saw that his face was a mask of polite civility as he spoke. "County Waterford, I should imagine? Lots of Powers in that area, aren't there?"

When Whitney looked back to Thomas Power, he was hunched, unmoving; his eyes narrowed suspiciously. Thrusting his head forward much like a turtle, he gave the younger man a thorough, brutal appraisal. "*Who* thinks?"

Michael nodded coolly, stepped up closer to the door, and offered his hand. "Michael Devlin, sir."

Ignoring the younger man's hand, Power's eyes narrowed even more.

One of the brackets that framed Michael's mouth

157

deepened. Letting his hand drop to his side, he said simply, "Belfast."

The old man's face exploded. His eyes fired with contempt, he sneered, "Hah! An Ulsterman!" Unbelievably, he spat at Michael's feet, barely missing the toes of his hiking boots.

Whitney swiveled toward Michael, grabbing his arm in an instinctive restraint.

He looked down at her, and she was amazed to see, not the fury she'd expected, but a glint of amusement. He glanced down at his boots, then back to her, patting her hand as if to reassure her. Only then did he turn to Thomas Power.

With a small shrug, he smiled cheerfully at the man and said, "Were you born here, Thomas Power, or did you come across?"

Power raked Michael's face with a fierce, measuring eye, his expression registering surprise at the younger man's aplomb. "Born on the Blackwater," he answered shortly. "Raised here."

Michael nodded and went on as smoothly as if he were carrying on a conversation with an old friend. "Live here alone, do you, Thomas?"

Power's long, blade-edged mouth remained closed.

"I see. We passed a cabin on the way, just down the road from you. Thought it might be your place for a moment, but Miss Sharyn said it looked abandoned. Have you no neighbors at all, Thomas?"

The older man condescended to shake his head. "My brother's place. He's dead."

"I'm sorry."

"Don't be. We couldn't stand the sight of each other."

Michael put a fist to his mouth and dipped his head. When he lifted his face to again meet Power's gaze, his features were deceptively bland.

"Well, Thomas, Miss Sharyn here has put herself at great inconvenience to drop by. Do you think we could at least come in and talk a bit?"

Power combed the younger man's face with a scathing look of contempt before turning to Whitney. After a long moment, he finally said, "She can. You can't."

Fascinated, Whitney watched Michael struggle to maintain his composure. It was obviously a battle, and she wouldn't have blamed him if he'd put the old man in his place.

Instead, he shifted his weight from one foot to the other, and with a slight lift of his chin said something wholly incomprehensible to Whitney.

Power's eyes sparked, then lost a fraction of their fire. His jaw, however, remained hard. "An Ulsterman with the Irish? I should think it would sour on your British tongue." He paused, then added, "I haven't heard it since my mam died, half my age ago. Never thought to hear it from a Brit."

Yes, he was definitely going to lose it now, Whitney saw, watching the slash of Michael's cheekbones turn crimson as his mouth thinned to a ruler-straight line.

Once more, Whitney watched him fight to control his irritation. He managed, but the glint of amusement that had been in his eyes earlier faded. He said something else that Whitney assumed to be in Gaelic, so strange were the shapes his lips formed.

When he'd finished, Power stared at him for a long, tense moment. Finally, pulling himself up into as straight a line as his crippled body could manage, he looked directly at Whitney and said, "I reckon the both of you can come in for a minute. But I don't have all day to chew the fat with you." Shooting another flinty look at Michael, he turned and, with obvious difficulty, shuffled back into the room.

"What in the world . . . did you say to him?" Whitney whispered as they followed the old man inside.

Smiling down at her, he answered, "The only thing I could think of that might pierce his armor. I simply told him—in Gaelic—that his mother, rest her soul, would be ashamed of his coarseness and his lack of hospitality." He paused, then explained. "We Irish, you see, pride ourselves on being a people of the open door. Even the American Irish, who were born here, tend to view hospitality not as a choice, but more as a way of life. I was counting on his remembering a few lessons learned at his mother's knee."

His eyes danced for a moment, and he leaned a little closer to her. "I also told him," he admitted, "that if he called me a 'Brit' one more time, I would see to it that the entire social services agency showed up on his doorstep in the morning."

They entered through a spartan kitchen—bare floor, wooden table flanked by two chairs, and a small, fifties' vintage stove. The cabin was surprisingly neat—rustic and rudely furnished—but clean.

Power led them into what was obviously a combination bedroom and sitting room. Against the far wall was a bed with a sagging middle, covered by a thin white chenille throw. A kerosene heater sat in the middle of the floor, and facing it was a large platform rocker with a thin cushion. On the opposite wall squatted a faded plaid, uncomfortable looking sofa.

There was no visible link to the outside world: no television set, no radio, no newspapers in sight. No frivolous souvenirs broke the austerity of the room; no family pictures gave it life or personality. The only hint that Thomas Power occasionally indulged himself in recreation was a small bookcase near the bed. Its shelves were crammed with a variety of books, all of which looked to be worn from use.

It was, Whitney thought with despair, the dwelling of a lonely, forgotten old man with a barren spirit.

They stayed for well over an hour, and in many ways,

Whitney thought, it was one of the saddest hours she'd ever spent. The more she learned about Thomas Power, the more she pitied him, though the very thought would have violated his precious independence.

He was far too proud for his own good, and it was the worst kind of pride, Whitney knew: a pride that views any offer of help as an invasion of privacy.

Power had lived alone all these years, had never married, had apparently never allowed anyone to share his life, even after the mine accident responsible for crushing his leg.

Whitney didn't miss how ill-at-ease he was with her, especially. At one point, she felt a sudden rush of sympathy for the old man. *Why, he's as awkward as a boy,* she realized. *It must make him miserably uncomfortable, having a woman in his cabin after all these years of being a bachelor.*

Though he had thawed somewhat toward them both by the time they rose to leave, he wouldn't budge from his refusal to accept assistance.

Standing at the door he had just opened for their departure, Whitney tried once more. "Mr. Power, it's not as if you'd be accepting charity."

He reddened. "You've got that right, miss. I've never taken a dime from no man, nor will I!"

"That's . . . what I'm trying to explain to you," Whitney said, her words tumbling out more quickly than usual. "It's entirely reciprocal—" she fumbled for a simpler word— "it's an *exchange* program, in a way. Someone helps you, and you help someone else. For example, I'm deaf, and—"

"Deaf?" Power leaned forward on his walker. "You can't hear?"

Whitney shook her head. "I read lips, Mr. Power. I can tell what you're saying . . . by watching you form your words."

He continued to study her. "I worked with a deaf-mute in the mines. He couldn't talk a lick. Talked on his hands, Uriah did." He stopped, then said, grudgingly, "You talk pretty good for someone who can't hear."

It was, Whitney realized, the nicest thing Power had said to her since she'd entered the cabin. She smiled at him with anticipation.

His next words, however, crushed her hopes that he might be softening. "Appreciate your coming all the way up here to talk to me. But I don't need none of what you're offering. It's not for me."

When Whitney started to speak, Michael touched her arm to stop her. She looked at him, reading his lips as he said to the old man, "Surely we can all use a bit of help from time to time, Thomas, don't you think?"

Power shot him a sour look, asking abruptly, "This your woman?"

Michael glanced at Whitney, and for a moment something flared in his eyes that caused an uncomfortable stirring inside her.

"She's my friend," he finally replied. "And you'd do well to let her be yours, Thomas."

The two men locked gazes for a long moment. Sensing the beginning of a duel, Whitney interrupted. "I'm sorry we imposed, Mr. Power," she said, pulling a calling card from her purse and handing it to him as she spoke. "We'll go now. But I wonder if I could at least have someone come by for you and bring you into town . . . for church on Sundays?"

He scowled. "I don't go to church."

"But if you'd like to—"

"I wouldn't," he said shortly. "I believe there's a God, mind. But I'm of the thought that a body doesn't need to be sitting inside a cold vault on a hard pew in order to keep in touch with their Maker."

Frustrated, Whitney frowned at him. "But, Mr. Power, . . . don't you think God wants us to know Him? To worship Him as a family? To get to know each other and help one

162

another?"

"Unlike some, miss," he replied with a sarcastic twist of his mouth, "I don't pride myself on knowing the mind of the Creator."

Out of the corner of her eye, Whitney saw Michael lift one dark brow in impatient exasperation. With a firm hand, he took her arm and turned her toward the steps. "If you change your mind, Thomas, you have Miss Sharyn's card." Not giving the old man time to reply, he propelled Whitney down the steps and back to the car.

Feeling a keen sense of failure, Whitney glanced back dejectedly over her shoulder.

Thomas Power had already closed the door.

Michael's only comment as they pulled away from the cabin was a caustic remark about the old man's stubbornness. After that, he seemed to turn all his attention to the scenery around them, some of the most rugged, untamed terrain in the county.

For her part, Whitney was too disappointed in the outcome of the trip to care about making conversation. She had found herself drawn to Thomas Power in spite of his abrasive rudeness. She was convinced that he was more than just a fiercely independent, stiff-spined old man who wouldn't admit he needed anyone. He was elderly, crippled, somewhat frail, and, most of all, lonely.

How did he handle the long mountain winters, she wondered, with his physical condition being what it was? Just getting himself in and out of a chair was an obvious effort. How did he get food? Medical supplies? She supposed some of the merchants in town delivered this far out, but what if there were an emergency? There was no way he could get off the mountain without help. Yet he apparently had no ties to the outside world, no family, no friends.

Lost in her anxious thoughts about the old man, she was surprised when Michael slowed the Bronco and bumped to a stop along the side of the road.

He turned to her, touching her shoulder. "Stop worrying about him," he said, leaning toward her. "There's nothing more you can do."

"Nobody should be that alone," she said worriedly.

"He chose his lifestyle, Whitney," he answered, not unkindly. "It wasn't forced on him."

She studied his face. "Sometimes . . . it seems that way, I know. But I don't believe for a minute that Thomas Power is happy, living . . . as he does. Circumstances created a pattern for him, and he allowed it to happen, that's true. But don't try to convince me that he's happy, Michael. We both know he's not. He's an angry, bitter, lonely old man who doesn't think there's hope for anything better."

"And is that how you see me, *alannah*? Unhappy, lonely—bitter?" His eyes searched her face.

Was he mocking her? She was never sure with this man. He could turn from iron to silk in a fraction of a second, making her head spin with confusion.

"Do you really want me to answer that, Michael?" she asked quietly.

He searched her eyes. "Why don't you?"

She met his gaze. "I . . . think you could easily end up that way, yes. Unless you allow yourself to need—and to be needed."

A muscle beside his eye jumped, and he turned away. As she watched, his jaw hardened for an instant, then relaxed. When he faced her again, the warm light of affection had returned to his expression. "And what if I should end up needing you, *alannah*? What then?"

Yes . . . what then? she asked herself, losing her breath at the look in his eyes.

Without warning, he did a lightning-fast mood shift. Tugging at her hand, he urged, "Come on—out! We're going to shoot some film. This is too grand to miss. Besides,

I have to work every now and again, you know."

His eyes laughing at her, he pulled her over the seat and out the door on his side, swinging her in the air for a moment before setting her down on the ground.

Retrieving his camera and binoculars from the back of the Bronco, he handed Whitney the Leicas, then dropped the camera strap around his neck.

He took her hand, gesturing toward a breathtaking drop-off a few feet away, to the right. "Let's go over there."

The air was much colder here than in the valley, sharp with the definite bite of late fall. Decaying leaves and moss made the ground spongy beneath their feet, and Whitney liked the way it felt as she walked. Breathing in the strong scent of pine and hardwood, she began to relax a little for the first time since early morning.

While Michael started to frame and shoot his pictures, Whitney studied the valley below through the high-powered binoculars. She could see for miles. The mountains formed a wraparound palette of late autumn colors: butterscotch and cinnamon-candy red, with random splashes of bronze and green. Hundreds of feet below, the entire valley was glazed in a shimmering, multicolored splendor.

Lowering the glasses, she gazed down at a fairly wide shelf only a few feet below where they were standing. It extended outward several feet before dropping off to a deadly, seemingly bottomless fall. She took an instinctive step backward, satisfied to simply watch Michael work.

He seemed a different person. He had become an artist: his camera a brush, the hills his canvas. Checking angles, adjusting for light, stooping and rising and pivoting back and forth, he was everywhere at once, moving with a fluid grace and a boyish exuberance that brought a smile to Whitney's face as she watched. She found it nearly impossible to reconcile this light-footed, energy-charged man in front of her with the other Michael Devlin—the man with the too-

165

distant eyes and the too-hard mouth.

Finally he stopped moving, bracing himself on the far edge of the roadside. Framed against a backdrop of rioting color, he hooded his eyes with his hand and stood gazing out over the sprawling valley. His face took on a look of infinite longing. Gone, at least for the moment, was the impassive stare, the stone mask, the impatient wariness. His eyes were yearning, his features vulnerable.

Abruptly he turned to smile at her. Whitney's heart skipped, setting off an alarm bell in her mind that she tried to ignore.

His face was flushed when he jogged over to her. Dipping his head and locking his gaze with hers, he said, "Let me take your picture. Please."

She started to shake her head, but he stopped her with the palm of his hand on her cheek. "Please," he said again. "I'll make only two prints: one for you, and one for me. I promise."

For a moment, Whitney almost wished he'd revert to the other Michael, the one with the grim face and the hard eyes. That Michael was far easier to resist. This Michael was too winsome, too charming, too easy to care about.

"Humor me; I'll trade you a steak dinner for two pictures." He dipped his head, smiling into her eyes. "Well?"

Apparently, he could sense her weakening. Raising his head, he glanced around them, scanning the hill on the other side of the road. "Over there, against that patch of wild flowers. It's a perfect backdrop for you."

Whitney looked in the direction he was pointing, then turned back to him. His eyes pleaded, and she surrendered.

"Two prints, Michael," she reminded him sternly. "That's all."

He held up his hand in good faith. "Let me just get a different filter," he said, heading for the car.

She watched him as he started back to her. He stopped for

166

a moment to fuss with the lens on the camera, then gave her a smile and came to take her arm.

"The light's perfect," he said, guiding her across the road. "I'll get a great shot over here." As they reached the other side, he inclined his head toward a spot against the hillside, saying, "Over there."

When she turned back to him, he was already focusing. "Yes, there. Can you still read my lips? All right, now lift your face a little. More. Look at me, Whitney." He made a quick adjustment. "Now, give me that wonderful smile of yours. Ah, yes, that's it . . . just . . . like . . . that." He shot the picture, lowered the camera and glanced around. "Let's go a bit further down for the next one."

"I thought you were only going to take one picture."

"I can see you don't know all you should about photography. It can often take an entire roll of film to get that one perfect shot. And I'm afraid I am something of a perfectionist."

He grinned at her mutter of disgust.

Still grumbling, she let him take her arm and hurry her down the road a few more feet. "Here. Over here among these flowers."

His gaze swept their surroundings, then Whitney, his eyes going over her hair and her outfit with a nod of approval. She was wearing a pastel lemon-colored sweater with ivory slacks. He reached among the flowers growing along the bank and plucked a long stem of goldenrod. "You should always wear yellow," he said, smiling as he handed her the flower.

His expression sobered, his gaze growing more intense as his hand lingered on hers for an instant longer than necessary. Whitney could see the conflict in his eyes as he continued to stare at her.

With one hand still holding hers, his other hand went to her shoulder. Gently, with great care, he pulled her into his

167

arms, watching her, drawing her, at last holding her.

Losing her breath, Whitney felt herself falling into his eyes, behind the mask, beyond the wall, into his heart. His lips touched her hair, then grazed her cheek. She had no idea whether she spoke his name aloud or simply thought it, but her mind began to hammer with the sound of it.

He put her away from him just enough that she could see his face, read his lips. "Whitney . . . *alannah* . . . you shine, do you know that? Every place you go, everything you touch, you make it shine. Sometimes I almost believe that you could make my life shine, too."

He framed her face with both hands. "Can you see yourself shining in my eyes, Whitney? Can you?"

She tried to speak his name, but the word on her lips was voiceless. He touched the corner of her mouth, then pressed his lips to the place he'd touched. Pulling back only a whisper's distance, his eyes questioned hers, then made the decision for both of them.

His kiss was tender, infinitely gentle, little more than a brief, fleeting touch. He released her slowly, with obvious reluctance. She felt his hands, the hands that always looked so large and powerful and confident, tremble on her shoulders as he stepped back from her.

They stood that way for a long moment, his eyes caressing her face, his expression both tender and uncertain.

"I care for you deeply, *alannah*," he finally said. "I have no right to feel this way for you, but I do."

"No right?" Whitney felt stunned, dazed by the depth of feeling she could read in his eyes.

"You're so—clean. I'm almost afraid I'll taint you with my touch."

Dismayed, she put her hand to his lips to silence him. "Don't."

"Whitney, you don't know me."

She smiled as she studied the lines of his face. "I think I

168

know the man you are. But you're still . . . obsessed with the man you used to be."

His eyes were troubled, his mouth tense. "They're the same."

She shook her head. "No, I don't think so. I think I know the . . . real Michael."

Was it fear she saw in his eyes an instant before he spoke again?

"There are things I have to tell you, Whitney. You won't feel the same about me when you know."

She sighed. "Michael, I've read the stories about what's happening in Belfast. I've seen the films on television. I know about . . . some of the things your police force has been accused of doing."

He paled, and once more she touched his cheek. "That's why you resigned, isn't it? That's why you left and came to the United States? Because you couldn't stand being a part of all that."

"That's true, yes. But it's not that simple, Whitney. That's not all of it—"

"The only thing I need to know is that you gave it up. That part of your life is over, Michael."

He closed his eyes, tight, then opened them. "There's more." As she watched, his face once again underwent a quicksilver transformation, shifting back to a look of strained resignation. "We'll talk tonight. There's a great deal I need to tell you. Much of it I should have told you before now, but I was waiting for—the right time."

Puzzled, she put her hand on his arm. "Michael?"

"Later. Not here. Come on, now, let me get this shot before we lose the light. The sun's already slipping."

He took two more shots, his demeanor reverting to professional detachment, then said, "Almost done. Let me have one more, right down there, close to that boulder."

Her pulse still racing and the goldenrod still in her hand,

169

Whitney turned and started walking. The road was steep, almost straight down. A patchwork quilt of dozens of different kinds of wild flowers checkered the hillside.

She stopped beside the boulder, waited until he focused her in the viewfinder and took a couple more shots.

A few yards to her right she spied the abandoned cabin they'd seen on the way up, the cabin that had belonged to Thomas Power's brother. It rested deep inside a thicket, surrounded by overgrown brush and shrubs. The windows were filthy, the siding unpainted.

She glanced at Michael, who was standing just up the road, doing something with his camera. Still shaken and confused by what had transpired between them, she turned and started trudging toward the cabin. There were tire tracks running parallel with the right side of it. She followed them until they veered off into a small glade that immediately narrowed and disappeared into the woods.

Uneasily, she realized that this particular setting was just right for snakes and other creatures she'd prefer to avoid, but curiosity overcame her misgivings as she forged ahead. She stubbed her toe once on a concealed rock, hesitated, then went on. The grass was dry, the bushes scratchy and laced with briars.

When she reached the porch, she stopped and examined the steps to make sure they looked safe. Satisfied, she took the half-dozen steps slowly and carefully, going to the front window to look in.

The pane was covered with dust and grime, but she thought she could make out the lines of a few pieces of furniture inside. She moved as close as she could to the window without actually pressing her face against the dirty glass. The interior was dim and shadowed, but she could see a table and what appeared to be a sagging couch.

She moved back. There was another window at the opposite end of the porch, and she started toward it. This one was smaller and more narrow. Cupping her hands at her temples to block the light, she squinted through the dusty glass.

She was looking into a bedroom. An old iron bed, covered with a blanket, was directly across from her. A chair sat beside it. She moved in still closer, smudging her face on the windowpane in order to get a better look. Frowning, she saw what appeared to be clothing laid out across the middle of the bed.

Her mind told her she was imagining it, that she couldn't possibly be seeing what she thought she was seeing. Heedless now of the dirty windowpane, she pushed her face against the glass and stared into the room.

Her eyes widened with growing horror and the goldenrod fell from her hand. She hadn't been mistaken. The clothing on the bed was exactly what she'd thought: a neatly arranged, black and white *Pierrot* costume.

17

It was incredible luck. Unbelievable. He couldn't have planned it to play any better. After all those months of scheming, acting, making himself out to be a rehab so those ridiculous doctors would let him out, it was finally over.

Even after he'd found her, it had taken another two weeks to come up with this place. He'd sensed all along that the success of his production might depend on staying out of sight, undiscovered, until he was ready to make his final appearance. The cabin was like a gift: close enough to town so he could come and go at will, far enough from people and traffic so he needn't worry about interference.

But to have her *delivered* to him like this, to have her just walk up on the porch like she was coming for a visit—it blew him away. He'd thought all along he would have to take her by force, grab her from her apartment or somewhere else.

It had been a wild shot, leaving that call on her machine yesterday. He'd been counting on her inability to say no to someone who needed help and thought the old duck up the road might be just enough to lure her up here. Even so, he'd thought it would be a case of having to force her off the road.

Instead, she was standing at the door, practically begging to come in.

Little Red Riding Hood—meet the big bad wolf...

He clamped his teeth down on his bottom lip to keep from laughing out loud.

His stomach pressed close to the ground, he inched forward a little more, moving just close enough to the edge of the rise so he could get a clear view of the man below.

The boyfriend. He hadn't counted on him being along. He'd wanted her alone, in her car. His hand caressed the gun at his side, then tightened on the butt as he stared down at the road. No matter. He'd take care of him, then her. *Two for one . . . both for me.*

Yeah, all the luck was swinging his way now. The proof was right in front of him. Right down there on the road. The jerk was just standing there, tinkering with the camera. An open target.

He couldn't see Whitney from here, but it didn't matter. She'd still be there, right where she was when he'd come across the back of the hill. Standing on the porch, peeping through the cabin windows. Nosy like always.

He had almost missed them. He'd kept an eye on the road all day, finally going inside long enough to get something to eat. The sound of a car engine had sent him back to the door to look outside. Sure enough, the Bronco had pulled off, just up the hill.

Now he wouldn't have to make another trip into town. If she hadn't shown on the hill today, he had planned to go back into town again tonight and hide in that upstairs storeroom while she was at her Wednesday night prayer meeting. Later, he could grab her and bring her out here to the cabin. He was tired of waiting. The play was losing its appeal.

But now the waiting was over. She had come to him. He didn't have to do a thing but get rid of the guy she was with and go down to the cabin to meet her.

The whole scenario was unreal. Beautiful.

He scooted up another inch, looking down at the dark head almost directly below him. The guy was wide open. He could blow his head apart from up here.

He smothered another laugh. Poor little Whitney wouldn't

173

even know what had happened. Down there at the cabin, she was too far off the road to see anything. He grinned. And for sure, she wouldn't *hear* anything.

By the time she realized her boyfriend had been wasted, it would be too late. She'd be where she belonged by then. Inside the cabin, with him.

His brain began to boil inside his head as he remembered all the months he'd lost because of her, the humiliation he'd suffered because of her. Everything that had gone wrong had been her fault. Stringing him on the way she had, pretending to be his lady all those weeks and then trying to drop him cold at the end. Because of her, he'd lost his job, lost his standing with the players club—just about lost his mind cooped up in that looney bin all those months.

She owed him, all right. She owed him plenty. And he didn't intend to wait any longer to collect.

He pushed off his stomach, got to his knees, hugging the gun to his side. Then he stood up, planted his feet, and aimed the .38.

The dark-haired man on the road below still had his head bent, studying the camera in his hands.

Suddenly, as if sensing movement above him, his head shot up, his hand sliding inside the field jacket at the same time.

He had a gun!

At the exact second Cory squeezed off his first shot, the guy on the road feinted left, firing as he pivoted to a crouch.

He started moving as soon as he saw the boyfriend go for his gun. Hitting the ground, he twisted and rolled behind a bush. Their bullets whistled and sliced air as they crossed.

The boyfriend made for cover behind a boulder near the road, but Cory got off another shot before he landed and this one hit its target. The guy yelled, throwing his arm up to the

174

side of his head, yelling, *"Whitney!"* Then he went down, slamming his head against a boulder as he fell.

Cory waited, then scrambled down the side of the hill. The guy was sprawled in the middle of the road. He flipped him over with the toe of his boot.

A narrow ribbon of blood trickled from his hairline, just above his ear. He was unconscious but alive.

He'd only nicked him. Probably the blow from the fall had done more damage. He aimed his gun to finish him, then lowered it again.

He'd take him back to the cabin first. From what he'd seen, Whitney and this guy had something going. It might be more interesting if he brought the boyfriend in on this. Every play should have an audience, after all. Sure. He'd keep him around for awhile, then finish him off later when it was time to take Whitney and get out.

Watching him closely, he stooped down and picked up the revolver that had been knocked from his hand by the fall. Pocketing the gun, he ripped the strap off the camera and used it to bind the guy's hands behind his back.

Then he straightened, staring down at the unconscious man with a measuring look. He could carry him; they were about the same size, except this guy was leaner. He decided against it. Shifting his gun to the other hand, he slipped his right arm under the man's bound hands, turned, and started to drag him down the road as if he were nothing but a large, cumbersome bag of laundry.

As soon as he turned, he saw her. She was standing in the middle of the road, staring up at him, wild-eyed with fear. She whirled around, apparently about to run in the opposite direction. Then, abruptly, she turned back as if she'd just realized what he was dragging· behind him.

When she started to run toward him, screaming at him as she came, he smiled and waved his hand—the hand holding the gun—in greeting.

18

Jennifer glanced at the clock on the dash as she passed the city limits sign. Almost 3:30. She'd promised Daniel to be back in town before 5:00; hopefully, it would be even earlier.

He'd given her a hard time when she called him from the station to tell him where she'd be. Not that she would have expected anything else. He liked to pretend that he didn't worry about her, that he respected her independence, but he worried, all right. *And I wouldn't have it any other way,* she smilingly admitted to herself.

Even after she'd explained that it would be easier for her to make a run up to Power's cabin and check on Whitney than to spend the afternoon worrying, the edginess had remained in his voice.

"Jennifer, Whitney is a grown woman—a mature, professional, extremely competent woman. She drives anywhere else she wants to go. Alone. You don't have to tailgate her."

"I'm not concerned about her *driving,* Daniel. That's not why I'm going."

"Then why *are* you going?"

When she fumbled for the words to make him understand, she realized that *she* didn't quite understand her feeling of unease. She thought it had as much to do with the peculiar way Whitney had been acting as with the treacherous road and Thomas Power's formidable reputation.

Making a right onto Holly Hill, she turned on the radio to get the station's 3:30 news. Lee Kelsey was already

176

into his report. She made a mental note to be sure his pay reflected all the overtime hours he'd been putting in lately.

"Law enforcement officials in Kentucky and surrounding states are on the lookout for a former mental patient released several weeks ago from a Kentucky facility for the criminally insane. Cory Ross, committed to the institution a little over a year ago after the brutal beating of a young deaf teacher in Louisville, was released on a probationary basis subject to a number of conditions . . . ."

Something caught at her heart, making it thud crazily, then race. She reached to turn up the volume, slowing the car for the stop sign just ahead at Blackwater Run.

" . . . Ross, now believed to be a suspect in at least three, possibly more, brutal slayings of young women in Kentucky, Indiana, and Ohio, failed to comply with the terms of his release by not appearing for his first outpatient counseling appointment, scheduled on a bimonthly basis. In addition, Ross is wanted for questioning in a number of random assaults on both male and female victims along the Kentucky-West Virginia border . . . ."

Her hands were shaking so violently on the wheel she could hardly keep the car under control. She knew she was losing part of the broadcast, knew she should be getting every detail, that it was important, but her mind insisted on isolating and replaying only a part of it over and over again. *" . . . a little over a year ago after the brutal beating of a young deaf teacher in Louisville . . . "*

Halfway up the hill, the car choked and rebelled against the steep grade. Downshifting, she tightened her grip on the wheel. The hill was straight up, the road narrow and pot-holed. The tension in her shoulders grew, matching the tight clench of dread around her heart. With an effort, she forced her attention back to Lee's voice.

" . . . The following description has been issued by the

Kentucky State Police. Ross is thirty years old; approximately five-foot eleven, one-hundred eighty-five pounds; dark blond hair; brown eyes; clean-shaven..."

Her eyes went to the forlorn little cabin on the right, and she slowed. She'd thought Thomas Power's place was farther up the hill, and there was no sign of Whitney's car. Still, there weren't that many cabins up here; she'd better stop and check. It could be that Whitney had already been here and gone, but she wanted to be sure.

When she spotted the Bronco several feet up on the other side of the road, she looked at it blankly for an instant, recognizing it immediately. *Devlin's car!* What was *he* doing up here? Where was Whitney?

Her pulse hammering, she twisted the wheel and jolted off the road, letting the engine idle in park. She sat unmoving for a long moment, her hands still locked on the steering wheel as she stared at the small, unpainted cabin half-hidden in the thicket. There was no sign of anyone inside or out.

"*... It is believed that Ross often relies on theatre costumes for disguise. One assault victim, who has tentatively identified Ross as her assailant, stated that he was wearing a black and white clown suit during the attack...*"

Tensing against a rush of panic, Jennifer turned off the engine, yanked her keys from the ignition, and got out of the car.

Daniel's hand shook as he set his half-full cup of coffee down on the kitchen countertop. Digging into the floor with his crutch, he hobbled to a stool, his attention still riveted on Lee's voice.

"*... State Police warn that Ross is probably armed and should be considered extremely dangerous. If you have any information regarding the suspect, please notify your local law enforcement agency immediately.*"

Shaken, his mind went into reverse, first locking on Whitney's attack the night of the Festival, then coming to rest on Jennifer's concern about her friend's "odd behavior," her withdrawal, her evasion.

With the help of the crutch, he pushed himself off the stool and went to the wall phone by the refrigerator.

Pushing the first memory button, the one programmed for the police, he waited. As soon as the dispatcher answered, he asked for Rick Hill.

Leaning heavily on the crutch, drumming the fingers of his free hand against the nearby countertop, he started talking as soon as the young officer answered the phone.

Hill knew Whitney's description of her assailant. He also knew about the interstate APB. In fact, as Daniel related Jennifer's concern about the "recent change" in Whitney, he began to get a sense that the policeman might know even more.

Abruptly, he stopped. "The man in the *Pierrot* suit—the one who attacked Whitney at the festival—it was Ross, wasn't it? And she was the . . . 'young deaf teacher' he attacked in Louisville." When Hill didn't answer right away, he pressed. "Rick?"

Daniel heard throat-clearing at the other end of the line. Then, "Dan . . . without breaking a certain confidence, I can't give you any details about how I got my information, but— yes. Miss Sharyn was the teacher in Louisville." There was a long sigh. "And if she *has* seemed—different—lately, she's had plenty of cause for it."

The anxiety that had begun to creep over Daniel at the beginning of the news broadcast hit full-force. "Rick," he interrupted shortly, "how about telling me about it in a patrol car?"

"What?"

Impatiently, Daniel explained about Whitney's trip out of

town and Jennifer's insistence on following her. "I don't have any concrete reason for thinking they might be in trouble, but if Whitney *is* in jeopardy in any way, then my wife is, too—because she's on the way out there. Rick, would you come and get me? As soon as you can."

"Dan, I'll take another man with me and go check—"

"I don't care how many men you take, Rick, so long as you take me, too." He paused. "Please."

Not waiting for an answer, he pressed the plunger to clear the line, then called his mother to see if she would meet Jason's bus and keep him with her until he got back.

19

Apprehensively, Jennifer climbed the steps and walked onto the porch. Standing just outside the front door, she listened, reluctant to knock, yet feeling a growing urgency about what might be going on inside the cabin.

What she heard drove a blade of fear straight through her heart.

The sound of Whitney's weeping was broken by a man's voice, rough and impatient as he snarled at her.

Attempting to control the fear that threatened to overwhelm her, Jennifer moved a little closer to the door, close enough that her ear actually touched the splintering wood.

The man suddenly quieted, but Whitney went on crying.

Unable to bear that heartbreaking sound—unable to think beyond the moment—Jennifer put her hand to the doorknob and started to twist.

The door exploded inward, hurtling her into the middle of a nightmare.

An iron-muscled arm swathed in black silk went around her throat, choking off her breath. She tried to scream, but the arm tightened even more against her windpipe.

"Shut up!" The man's voice was heavy and coarse with rage.

Directly across from her, in the middle of the room, Whitney sat on a chair at a square, battered table. Her hands were bound behind her. An open makeup kit lay on top of the table in front of her. Beside it was a swivel mirror.

For one horror-filled moment, she met Jennifer's gaze.

The enormous eyes staring at her, the eyes Jennifer had always thought so hauntingly beautiful, were now sunken pools of anguish in a white mask. The perfect features had been painted with clown white. The delicate mouth was a grotesque red slash. Black paint from the weeping eyes tracked dark paths all the way down each side of her face.

Jennifer cried out and tried to lunge forward, but a calloused hand smeared with white makeup went over her mouth, and she was pushed, hard, onto a chair at Whitney's right.

She looked up. Slumped in a chair at the opposite end of the table, his head lolling weakly forward, his hands also bound behind him, was Michael Devlin. Stunned, Jennifer saw that a ribbon of blood furrowed the left side of his face, and a darkening bruise shadowed his temple on the right. His eyes were open but not fully focused. The collar of his field jacket was stained with blood. On the table in front of him were his keys, his wallet, and what remained of his camera.

Jennifer made herself look up at the man standing beside her with a gun pointed at her head.

"Don't move, chick. Don't even breathe."

He wasn't overly tall, but in spite of the billowing *Pierrot* costume, Jennifer could tell that he was heavily muscled. His eyes were cold obsidian and conveyed a brutal kind of power. His face was covered in clown white—like Whitney's—with the same exaggerated red mouth and black paint accenting his eyes. He was chewing gum in a hard, driving rhythm.

Jennifer's heart tripped and began to pound painfully against her rib cage as she stared into the malevolent, painted face of Cory Ross.

"I suppose you just happened to be in the neighborhood," he sneered.

182

She twisted on the chair, and he rammed the gun against the side of her head. "Don't—move."

After an excruciatingly long moment, he pulled the gun back no more than an inch. "Where's the hulk?"

"Wh-what?" Jennifer blinked, swallowing hard.

"Your old man. The blind boy."

Anger flared, but she fought the urge to turn on him. "Laid up, is he?"

Something in his voice made her glance up at him. His expression was amused, gloating.

She knew then who was responsible for Daniel's broken leg. She stiffened, grinding her teeth so hard her jaw began to ache.

Devlin's head came up slowly. He shook it as if to banish the fuzziness. His eyes rolled, and Jennifer could see him fighting to focus them. Gradually, they cleared and locked with hers in a look that held both fury and despair.

Ross reached across the table for a length of rope that lay in front of Whitney. Tucking the gun under his arm, he bound Jennifer's hands, securing them to the back of the chair behind her.

He straightened, pulled the gun from beneath his arm, and leveled it once more at her head.

"The blind man know where you are?" he asked abruptly.

Unable to speak, Jennifer simply stared at the dark opening of the barrel.

Watching her with a measured smile, Ross touched the cold tip of the gun barrel to her lips. Jennifer shuddered but forced herself not to flinch. For several seemingly endless moments, she sat frozen by fear.

"Doesn't matter," he murmured sarcastically, finally breaking the silence. Cracking his gum, he added, "The blind man doesn't worry me."

Taking the gun off her, he walked across the room to a sagging couch and laid the .38 beside another revolver.

Coming back to the table, he directed his words to Jennifer but kept his eyes on Whitney. "Well, since you're here, I suppose we'll have to find a part for you."

"What?" Jennifer looked at him numbly.

Still watching Whitney with the same calculating smile, he answered, "A part, chick. A part in my play. Whitney and I have the leads, so you and the shutterbug here will just have to settle for supporting roles." He turned to her then, and, staring up into his hideously made-up face, Jennifer felt as if she had just come face to face with a raw, deadly evil.

He whirled around, turning his attention on Devlin. Appraising the wounded photographer with hard eyes, he reached for the wallet on the table.

"Something bothers me about you, shutterbug," he said, his eyes never leaving the journalist's face as he began to yank bills and cards from his wallet and toss them randomly on the table. "I'm trying to figure out why you'd pack a .357 Magnum with your camera. You wouldn't want to explain that to me, would you?"

He glanced down at the billfold, frowning as he pried something out of the concealed bill compartment. Staring at the laminated card in his hand, his marble-cold eyes turned hot with anger as he shifted his gaze to Devlin.

Without warning, he slapped the card on the table, then swung an arm out and grabbed the journalist by his hair, yanking his head back, hard.

Devlin uttered a startled cry of pain, and his face turned ashen.

"Cory—don't!"

At Whitney's outburst, Ross turned to her without releasing his grip on Devlin. "Shut up!"

Picking the card up off the table, he waved it in front of the injured man's face, roaring at him. "Where's your shield, cop?"

He dipped his head to a level with Devlin's, still holding

184

him by the hair. *"Cop!"* He made the word an obscenity.

Releasing Devlin's hair, he shoved his hand roughly into the blood-stained field jacket, patting down the lining. When he freed his hand from the coat, he was holding a badge.

He glanced from the ID card to the badge for a long, silent moment before flinging them onto the table.

"I *knew* you had a stink on you!" he shouted. "I was smelling *cop!"*

Her eyes shifting wildly between the two men, Whitney again cried out. "Cory, no! He's not a policeman anymore! He's—"

"—*a detective!* A *Cincinnati* detective!" he hissed furiously. He grasped Devlin by the back of the neck, slamming him face-down on the table hard enough to lift the chair off the floor as it pitched forward.

Devlin groaned, and Ross again snapped his head back by the hair. "What's your name, cop? What are you doing here? And don't tell me you're just *moonlighting!"*

Devlin's eyes went to Whitney, who was staring at him with wounded disbelief. "Michael?"

His eyes pleaded with her as he shook his head miserably. "I was going to explain, *alannah* . . . I was going to tell you tonight—"

"Then it's true?" she interrupted him. "You're . . . a detective?"

Nodding, he continued to beg her with his eyes.

Whitney stared at him, her expression hurt and confused.

Jennifer didn't understand what was happening. A part of her wanted to strike the man across from her for causing that sudden, terrible look of pain in Whitney's eyes, while at the same time she rebelled against the abuse he was suffering at Ross's hands.

"Why did you lie to me?" Whitney's question was an indictment.

185

"I didn't—exactly lie, *alannah*—"

"Don't call me that!"

He shook his head in defeat.

"What was I, Michael?" she asked in a choked voice. "Your *bait*?" Her eyes raked his face accusingly.

He looked at her. "No! *Alannah*—"

"Don't *call* me that!" she screamed at him, tears coursing down her cheeks, shattering her face into a pathetic visage of destruction.

He looked away from her, saying nothing.

Ross, who had been listening to the exchange in menacing silence, broke into the conflict. "This is good material, but I'm afraid we'll have to trash it for now." Bracing the palms of both hands on the table, he eyed the detective. "Let's just get to the nitty-gritty, all right? What, exactly, is *Detective* Michael Tierney from Cincinnati doing in Shepherd Valley, West Virginia?"

Jennifer frowned as both she and Whitney, almost in unison, repeated, *"Tierney?"*

Ross looked from one woman to the other, his eyes narrowing.

Michael's gaze was fixed on Whitney. "My last name is *Tierney*. *Devlin* is my middle name."

Whitney's look plainly said that she felt betrayed.

"What are you, anyway?" Ross snapped. "You're not American, are you? How can you be a cop when you're not even an American?"

"I came here from Northern Ireland," the detective answered evenly. "I'm an American citizen."

"I'm an American citizen," Ross mimicked. "Why don't you learn to talk like one, then, cop?" He moved a little closer to Michael. "You're here because of me, right?"

Michael lifted his face and shot a look of contempt at the other man, but said nothing.

"Talk to me, Irish. I asked you a question."

The detective hesitated. Jennifer got a sense of a terrible kind of anger emanating from him, but as she watched, he seemed to gain control and subdue it.

When he answered Ross, his voice was impassive. "I'm part of an interstate investigation."

"And what, exactly, are you investigating, Irish?" The white makeup made Ross's eyes look as dark—and hard—as chunks of coal.

When the detective didn't answer, Ross's hand again snaked out and seized his hair. "I said *talk*, cop!"

Michael grimaced at the pain but remained silent.

Unexpectedly, Ross released the detective. His tone was deceptively quiet when he said, "Never mind. We both know what you're investigating, don't we, Irish?"

Michael's reply was a hard stare.

"Yeah, we know," Ross said with a shrug. "Doesn't matter anyway. You're history."

Turning his back on the detective, he came to stand beside Jennifer's chair.

She cringed inwardly, steeling herself not to shrink from him when she felt his eyes on her. Something about the man made her skin crawl; she thought that if he touched her, she might start screaming and never stop.

Startled, she felt him begin to untie her hands.

"Don't get excited, chick," he said with a dry laugh as he freed her from the chair. "This is only temporary. You're coming with me for a minute."

"Wh-where?"

"Hey!" He turned on her, his face a white-painted abomination. "This is *my* play! You don't ask any questions."

Jennifer's gaze went to the detective, who gave her a small shake of his head and a look of warning.

"Get up!" Ross yelled at her, reaching across the table for Michael's keys.

She did as he said, momentarily grasping the edge of the table to steady herself. Her stomach was cramped from tension and fear, and she doubled over for a moment with pain.

Ross yanked her arm behind her, and started hauling her backward across the floor. Reaching the couch, he bent sideways to pick up one of the guns.

"We're going to get rid of her car and get that Bronco out of sight," he said, his breath hot and sour at the side of Jennifer's face. "And the two of you are going to sit right where you are until we come back."

His voice was thick and menacing. "If either one of you so much as scoots an inch away from that table, I'll blow your snoopy friend here all over the mountain. This'll only take a couple of minutes, Whitney-love. When I come back, you can put on your costume, and we'll do a little rehearsing. Irish and your buddy here can be our audience."

Whitney cast another look of terror at Jennifer, then dropped her head and looked away.

Now clutching her arm, Ross pocketed his own gun before picking up the Magnum and pressing the tip of its barrel against Jennifer's cheek. "Don't worry, chick. Irish will do as he's told. He knows exactly what this .357 will do to a pretty lady's head, don't you, cop?"

Again yanking her arm behind her, he flung the door open and backed out onto the porch. "Where's your keys?"

"M-my jacket pocket," Jennifer stammered, reaching with her left hand to pull them out. At her movement he wrenched her arm even harder, and she cried out against the pain.

"I'll tear it off if you don't shut your mouth!" he shouted at her.

When they reached the bottom step, he released her, giving her a shove toward the Honda. "We'll pull it back there in the woods with mine," he said, motioning to a dense grove of trees behind the cabin.

He pushed her behind the steering wheel, then ran around to get in on the passenger's side, pointing the gun at her as soon as he hit the seat.

Her mind began to spin. She tried desperately to think of something she could do to get away from him. If she could somehow break free, she could get help for Whitney and Devlin—*Tierney*. But the man had two guns and out-weighed her by a good seventy pounds. Tears of hopeless-ness stung her eyes as she put the key in the ignition. There was nothing she could do. Nothing.

"Don't try anything cute, chick," he said, smiling at her through the blood-red slash that framed his mouth. "You might want to keep in mind that you're the most expendable member of this troupe."

Whitney could feel Michael's eyes on her after Cory dragged Jennifer from the room. She saw him dip his head toward her, knew he was trying to force her to look at him. But she wouldn't. She couldn't bear the pain.

Somehow she knew that the torture she was feeling at this moment was much worse than any physical punishment Cory would eventually inflict on her. She had never known that the agony of betrayal could be such a consuming, annihilating pain.

Out of the corner of her eye, she saw his movement, knew he was willing her to turn toward him.

Unable to help herself, she looked at him.

His eyes were burning with an urgency that caught and held her. "I know you're angry . . . hurt. And you've a right. But you must understand why I did what I did." He shifted, wincing as if the movement caused him pain. "Whitney, don't you see, I was afraid that if you knew too much, it would go worse for you if Ross got to you. That he'd think you'd—conspired with me. Whitney, don't look away. Please."

189

There was blood on one side of his face. All the way down. And a terrible bruise on the other side. She wanted to touch the bruise, clean away the blood. She wanted to heal him. She wanted to hit him.

"Whitney? Remember, I told you there were things you had to know, that we'd talk tonight. I was going to tell you everything—and then find somewhere else for you to stay."

At her puzzled frown, he explained, "When I went upstairs to the storeroom today—to see about the leak—I found Ross had been up there."

A wave of cold fear washed over her. "Upstairs?"

Michael nodded. "There were gum wrappers scattered all over. And someone had carved on the floor with a pocket knife. It looked as though someone . . . someone under stress . . . had been . . . killing time." He stopped, hunching a shoulder as if to ease the stiffness from it. "I knew I couldn't let you spend another night in that house as long as he was free. I would have told you the truth tonight, Whitney. I intended to take you somewhere where you'd be safe, under round-the-clock police protection until we brought Ross in."

His eyes roamed her face with a look of appeal. "Whitney, when this is over—don't look at me like that, it *will* be over—I promise you I'll explain everything. There's no time now. I want you to do exactly what Ross tells you. I know you're frightened, but I think you can keep yourself alive by not angering him. Whitney . . . he's killed at least three women that we're sure of, perhaps others. Assaulted and beaten even more, we think."

Feeling sick, she watched him moisten his cracked lips and pull in a deep breath.

"He's a psychopath, Whitney. He's insane, you already know that. His mind is hanging by only the weakest of threads. If you defy him, he may explode. This is all a play to him—an obscene, mad play. You must pretend to play your part. Do exactly what he tells you to do. Don't cross him. Don't anger him. Don't even question him. Just—pretend with him."

She shook her head hopelessly. "It won't help. He's going to kill me..."

"No!" Michael pushed his head as far forward as he could, his eyes blazing. "You can buy time for yourself—for all of us—by playing his game. Time is what we need, Whitney."

"You don't know him, you..."

His face changed, tightening to a hard mask that made her flinch. "I know him. All too well. I know what he's done... I know his victims... I know the extent of his depravity. I've lived with his madness, studied it, for over a year now, just so I could trap him."

She lifted her chin defiantly. "And you used me for bait. You lied to me."

He shook his head. "No, not altogether. I *am* a photojournalist—at least a part-time one. It was a hobby for a long time. It's my way of dealing with the stress of the job, you see. Then a couple of years ago some of my stuff was published. I've been selling to the nationals fairly regularly ever since."

"But you came here because you thought I'd lead you to Cory?" she persisted.

He nodded. "I don't deny that. He became an obsession with me. One of his victims was a young girl, a student at the University of Cincinnati. He beat her to death."

Whitney uttered a soft cry of despair.

Pain glazed his eyes as he went on. "She was my partner's niece. I saw what Ross did to her. I couldn't forget it. At the time, we didn't have a clue as to who murdered her. We began studying the sheets, found an *m.o.* running through two other fatal beatings—one in Louisville, another in Indiana. I started building a file, working with an interstate team. When I learned about Ross being locked up after your

191

beating, I spent several days in Louisville. By the time I left, I was sure I'd found my man."

He pressed his lips together, tightened them, then continued. "Every instinct I had told me Ross was the lunatic we were looking for. But I had to prove it. I kept on with the investigation in my spare time, all those months he was in the hospital. When he was released, I asked for a leave. I wanted to build an absolutely airtight case against him. By then I was convinced he'd go after you. He can't take even a hint of rejection, you see. He simply goes berserk. You already know that."

When she nodded, he said, "He's even worse now. He's a raving savage if he's crossed. Anyway," he went on, "I knew he'd come after you. There was no way he'd let you get away with rejecting him and then testifying against him."

"How . . . did you find me?"

He shrugged. "It wasn't that hard. Most people don't have the least idea how many loose ends they leave behind when they try to disappear. Once I'd found you, it was just a matter of waiting for him to show."

"So you *were* . . . using me," she accused him quietly.

His eyes searched hers for a long moment before he answered. "In a way. But I was also trying to save your life." He swallowed, then added, "And perhaps mine."

At her puzzled look, his features softened, and he managed a faint smile. "Read my lips, Whitney. If I don't have the chance to tell you anything else, I want you to know this much. It isn't the way I'd choose to tell you, but it's the truth, nevertheless."

As he spoke, his face, haggard and pain-shadowed, began to relax, just a little.

"The first time I looked at your picture," he said, "I saw something in your eyes. I had no idea what it was, only that it was something I had to find. As mad as it sounds, I saw something looking out at me from your eyes that was almost

192

like a touch of healing. I began to think if I could find you, I might find—" he stopped, shaking his head uncertainly, "—I don't know what exactly." He looked at her. "Hope, perhaps. Healing . . . I'm not sure."

Bewildered, she searched his eyes.

"I didn't understand it either, *alannah*—please let me call you that—it almost frightened me. I—just knew I couldn't live with myself unless I found you and tried to give you your freedom from Ross. I know now that I was counting on gaining my own freedom as well."

Whitney could only look at him, confused, wanting to understand . . . wanting to believe.

"Whitney . . . I can't touch you, but look at my eyes. A man should touch a woman when he tells her he loves her. My eyes are touching you, Whitney. My heart is touching you. I love you, *alannah*. I think I've loved you since the first time I held a photograph of you and looked into those incredible eyes of yours. I love you. And I . . . need you. I need you to love me. I think . . . if you'll allow me to love you . . . and if you can love me back, perhaps in time I can learn—to love other people as well. The way you love. Whitney, if you don't believe anything else, believe that."

She *did* believe him. The truth was written on his face. And, oh, how she longed to be able to give him the healing he'd been so desperately searching for.

She squeezed her eyes shut. *But I can't, Lord . . . I can't. Only you can give that kind of healing. Oh, my dear, dear Lord, whatever happens . . . heal him . . . heal his lonely heart, his anguished spirit . . . heal him with your love . . . please . . . become Lord of his life, too.*

She opened her eyes. "I believe you, Michael."

They were still holding each other close with their eyes when the door flew open.

Ross came whirling through it, waving his gun, shoving Jennifer across the room with a force that sent her flying

193

against the table. He was shaking with anger, screaming something too fast and too wild for Whitney to catch.

It was Michael who mouthed the words to let her know what was happening.

"There's a police cruiser outside," he said, his eyes on Ross and the gun.

20

Jennifer pushed herself off the table, stunned by the fury of Ross's violence.

He was standing in the middle of the room, screaming maniacally at all of them.

"She called the cops!" He shot a wild-eyed look of rage at Jennifer. "A patrol car just came down the hill! Two cops and her old man!"

Hugging her arms to her chest, Jennifer backed away from Ross, praying that the fact the police car was coming *down* the hill meant that they'd already checked Thomas Power's place and, not finding Whitney there, would look for her here.

Not taking his eyes off Ross, who was staring at the closed door as if he thought it might crash open at any moment, Michael silently mouthed the words to Whitney.

"Two policemen—and Daniel."

A look of hope flared high in her eyes and held.

Jennifer stepped backward, moving alongside Whitney's chair and giving her shoulder a quick squeeze.

Ross whipped around. *"You—"* He shouted an oath at Jennifer, then streaked across the room to the window. His back to the wall, he peered out the side of the dusty glass, watching.

As if he'd only then remembered that Jennifer was still unbound, he turned to her. "Get on that chair—where you were before! I don't want you moving, I don't want you *breathing!*" When she hesitated, he screamed, *"Do it!"*

Jennifer vaulted to the chair, turning just enough to watch Ross out of the corner of her eye.

He began to ramble almost irrationally. Dread scraped the nape of her neck, sending a tremor down her back. What would happen to the three of them if Ross went completely out of control?

" . . . didn't even get the Bronco out of sight . . . now we can't have our play . . . they're spoiling everything . . . now we'll have to leave and go somewhere else . . . "

Jennifer looked at the detective across from her. His eyes were hard, fixed on Ross with a watchful look of speculation.

Everyone but Whitney jumped when a voice suddenly came across the patrol car's loudspeaker.

"Ross, this is the police. Come out before anyone gets hurt. We've got you covered—drop your weapon and come out."

Jennifer screamed when Ross shattered the windowpane with his gun and shouted, "Listen up! I've got three people in here—two women and a cop—and there's not a one of them coming out alive unless I walk. You got that?"

There was silence for a moment, then another voice cut in. *"Ross—this is Daniel Kaine."*

Jennifer's hand went to her mouth as she choked off a cry.

"You've got my wife in there. Listen to me. I'm blind, and I'm on crutches. I'm no threat to you. Send the women out and let me come in."

"No!" Jennifer gasped, shooting up off her chair. "Daniel—"

Without turning, Ross yelled at her. "Shut up!"

For a long moment, there was silence in the cabin and on the road. Then the sound of tires squealed as another car came sliding up the road.

"State police!" Ross choked out. He whirled around, and Jennifer caught her breath at his face. Perspiration had splotched the white makeup. The black paint around his eyes was smeared from rubbing. The red gash that was his

196

mouth was open and panting.

Her blood seemed to slow and freeze as she stared at him. He looked—inhuman.

Unexpectedly, he veered away from the window and crossed the room, waving the gun in their direction as he backed up to the open doorway that led into the other room.

"Don't move," he warned them.

The three of them watched as he continued to back off into the adjoining room. Keeping the gun as well as his gaze leveled at them, he yanked something off the bed, tossing it at Michael as he charged back into the room.

Hurriedly, he hoisted the gun under his arm and untied the detective.

"Stay put, don't even blink," he mumbled, pulling the rope away with trembling hands.

As soon as the rope dropped away from Michael's hands, Ross straightened, aiming the gun at Whitney's head.

"Put that on," he told the detective, motioning to the black and white *Pierrot* costume he'd thrown at him. "Just pull it over your clothes—hurry up, get it on! Try anything and I blow her out the window!"

Michael moved, grimacing at the pain when he hauled himself out of the chair. Without a word, he pulled the ballooning clown pants over his jeans, yanked the tunic over his head, then pulled the skullcap down over his hair.

"Do your face," Ross ordered shortly, motioning to the makeup kit. "Fast!"

When the detective hesitated, glancing from the man with the gun to the makeup, Ross pushed the gun against the back of Whitney's head. *"Move, cop!"*

Jennifer felt the Irish policeman's fury as he smeared the clown white over his face with a surprisingly steady hand, then swabbed the red greasepaint around his mouth, finally rimming his eyes with black.

197

She glanced at Whitney. As soon as she saw the look in her eyes and the tears spilling down her painted cheeks, she ached for her friend's hopeless look of love.

"All right," Michael said matter-of-factly. "How's this?"

Ross seemed to quiet a little as he appraised the other man's appearance. Then he nodded. "Not bad for an amateur."

Jennifer felt herself move one step closer to hysteria at the emotionless exchange between the two men.

Ross went back to the shattered window. "Okay, cops. You give me free passage, I'll bring everyone out. Otherwise, they're all dead. I'll shoot them first, then myself. What's it going to be?"

After a long silence, a voice Jennifer recognized as Rick Hill's came over the loudspeaker. *"What do you want, Ross?"*

"I go to the Bronco—nobody moves until I get inside and drive down the hill." He waited, breathing heavily, eyeing the three at the table as he pointed the gun at them.

Silence. Then, *"All right, you've got it. Send the two women out first, and nobody touches you."*

He moved to untie Whitney, pulling her up from the chair and holding her captive with an arm lock around her neck.

He pointed the gun at Jennifer. "Go."

Tears shimmering in her eyes, Jennifer fastened one last, lingering look on Whitney. Then she turned and went out the door, her legs shaking so violently she prayed she'd make it off the porch without falling.

She ran toward the police cars, only vaguely aware of the buzzing activity taking place between the two city policemen and the state police. She saw only Daniel, propped on his crutch, leaning against the side of the cruiser. His face was haggard, his expression stricken.

As soon as he heard her cry his name, he pushed himself

away from the car and began to move toward her.

From inside the patrol car, Sunny began to bark fiercely but Daniel didn't seem to hear.

Reaching him, Jennifer threw her arms around his waist and held him. For a moment, she could do nothing but sob helplessly. Then she turned to Rick Hill. "Ross doesn't have any intention of letting Whitney go! He's going to take her with him, if you let him get away! And he'll *kill* Michael Devlin—he's a policeman!"

The officer's quiet, level voice steadied her. "We know, Mrs. Kaine. What about weapons? What has Ross got?"

"Two guns." Another thought struck her. "Ross has on a—a clown suit!" she choked out. "And he made Michael put on one just like it. You won't be able to tell them apart when they—"

The words died in her throat as she saw the slender policeman's face pale. With her arms still locked around Daniel's middle, Jennifer turned to look toward the cabin.

Both men, identical in the black and white *Pierrot* costumes, had appeared on the porch. Whitney was between them, each man holding her by the arm.

Jennifer heard a soft groan of frustration from a nearby state policeman as the trio came down the steps and began to walk toward the road. "Which one is *which*? We can't risk shooting."

They were halfway to the cars when one of the *Pierrots* let go of Whitney and shoved her forward.

"Run, Whitney!" he shouted at her, then whirled around and threw himself at the other clown.

Rick Hill drew his gun with one hand, running toward Whitney to pull her to safety with the other.

One of the state policemen immediately joined them. Pushing Whitney behind him, he blocked her with his body.

As the *Pierrots* scrambled in the brush, one of them pulled a gun from beneath his tunic.

The unarmed clown high-kicked the gun, sending it flying into the brush several feet away. At that, the other clown bolted across the road, running uphill in the direction of the parked Bronco. The other followed in fierce pursuit.

Rick Hill turned to Whitney, touching her shoulder to get her attention.

"Can you tell them apart, Miss Sharyn? Do you know which man is Detective Tierney?"

"You know his real name?" Jennifer blurted out with surprise.

The policeman looked at her. "Yes, ma'am. We've known from the beginning—since he arrived in town. We've been working together on this."

Whitney clutched his arm. "I can't tell, not from here. Take me closer."

The state policeman in front of her turned. "No, ma'am. You've got to stay right where you are."

Leaving Whitney with one officer, the two city patrolmen and the other state policeman began to move up the road, weapons ready, covering the two *Pierrots* who were now wrestling on the ground in front of the Bronco.

Jennifer felt Whitney move. She cried out, but before she could stop her, Whitney was flying across the road and running up the hill toward the *Pierrots*.

Jennifer started after her, but the state policeman put a firm hand to her arm. "I'll get her. Stay with your husband." Immediately, he took off across the road, his gun ready as he raced up the hill behind Whitney.

Jennifer clung to Daniel, watching. Suddenly she saw another gun in one of the *Pierrot's* hands. "There's the other gun!" she cried out. Daniel's arm tightened around her shoulder.

"Oh, no—she's going right to them!"

Daniel held her as she tried to pull free. "You can't *do* anything, Jennifer! You'll just make it harder for the police." He pulled her even tighter against his side.

Both *Pierrots* were now on their feet, dangerously close to the edge of the cliff as they struggled for the gun.

Horrified, Jennifer saw Whitney suddenly turn and head directly for the rim of the drop-off, stopping no more than a foot away from the edge. She hesitated, turned to the police, then back to the struggling clowns, shouting, "*Michael*, help me! Help me!"

Moving right to the edge of the cliff, she tottered as she looked down.

The clowns turned, one with a gun in the air, the other in a crouch as he struggled to keep his footing. Two stunned, bewildered white faces stared at Whitney. Then one bolted and started to run, crying her name as she plunged over the edge.

The *Pierrot* with the gun aimed at the running man and fired. Grabbing his shoulder, the wounded *Pierrot* didn't stop. He glanced down when he reached the rim of the drop-off, then straightened and jumped over.

Jennifer screamed and broke free of Daniel's arms. He tried to call her back, but she went on, reaching the road just as another shot rang out. Looking up the hill toward the Bronco, she saw the *Pierrot* with the gun fall to the ground.

She reached the edge of the cliff and dropped to her knees, crying so hard she could scarcely get her breath as she looked over.

Stunned, her sobs stopped abruptly as she stared at the scene below in disbelief. Only a few feet beneath her, in the middle of a shelf-like extension, the injured *Pierrot* was holding Whitney in his arms.

Jennifer stared at them for a long moment. She started to call out, then stopped. She continued to gaze down at them for another instant. Finally, assured of their safety, she pulled back to give them some privacy.

As she turned away, she couldn't help but hear Michael's unsteady voice. "That was a daft thing to do! You could have been killed! Whatever made you try such an idiotic stunt?"

There was silence for a moment. Then, "I had to make sure the police wouldn't shoot the wrong man."

At his muffled exclamation of bewilderment, Whitney explained. "I had to get you away from Cory, to separate you so the police would have a chance at him. I had to do *something*. Something that would prove who you were. It was the only thing I could think of." She paused. Then, "I knew you knew about the shelf . . . that it would break my fall."

"I *forgot* about the shelf! I forgot *everything* when I saw you going over that cliff!"

"But you jumped anyway," she replied after a moment. "You meant it, didn't you, what you told me the night you put the lamp in my front window?"

"What?" The word was gruff, his voice still unsteady.

"That if I ever needed you . . . you'd come to me."

He missed only a beat before Jennifer heard him say, "Yes. And you were equally certain, of course, that all those policemen out there would know it as well?"

There was only the briefest pause before Whitney answered him. "Michael Devlin Tierney, I should think you, of all people, would have faith in a fellow officer's ability to tell the good guys from the bad guys."

When the statement went unanswered, Jennifer moved to hold off the approaching policemen for at least another moment.

Epilogue

From her place in the choir loft, Jennifer looked out over the crowded, candlelit auditorium, searching for those faces most familiar and dear to her.

Jason was easy to find, huddled closely between his grandparents, Lucas and Pauline. Jim Arbegunst, the adopted teenage son of Daniel's parents, was there, too, on the other side of his mother. Both boys caught Jennifer's eye and grinned at her, Jason waving the small candle he'd be lighting later in the service.

Gabe and Lyss were in the choir loft. Lyss and Jennifer were seated side by side as usual; Gabe was at the end of the row.

Glancing nervously over to the organ, she wondered where Daniel was. He was supposed to play the last 15 minutes of the pre-service music, and he wasn't there yet.

A stirring in the back of the shadowed auditorium caused a few heads to turn, and Jennifer craned her neck to see what was going on.

At the same time, she sensed movement out of the corner of her eye, and sighed with relief as Daniel and Sunny came down the far aisle.

As he always did, Daniel smiled up at the choir loft in her direction. With Sunny sitting quietly beside the organ, he slid onto the bench and began to play soft, traditional Christmas carols.

Reassured, Jennifer turned her attention to the back of the middle aisle. As she watched, Thomas Power moved into the light, approaching slowly, but with obvious dignity, on his walker. Holding his right arm was Whitney. Obviously, it was Thomas Power's presence that was creating all the stir. To Jennifer's knowledge, he'd never been inside the church building. Not that the townspeople hadn't tried. Until Whitney and Michael had marched into his life, however, the solitary old miner had resisted every effort to draw him into the community and the church family. Directly behind the two of them walked Michael, apparently on duty tonight since he was wearing his uniform.

Michael Tierney was a brand new addition to the Shepherd Valley City Police Department—and, according to the talk around town, a real "catch" for their small community. Of course, he'd made no secret of the fact that he had fallen in love with the town almost from the first week.

Smiling, Jennifer mused that his love for Shepherd Valley took second place to his overwhelming love for Whitney Sharyn—who on New Year's Eve would become Mrs. Michael Tierney.

The three of them reached the front of the church, and while Michael helped the elderly man to get settled in the pew behind the Kaines, Whitney reached over to tousle Jason's hair.

Sitting there, waiting for Daniel to end the last carol before the start of the service, Jennifer made eye contact with Whitney and smiled. Michael, too, looked up and nodded with a grin.

What an incredibly handsome couple they make, Jennifer thought, her smile widening. Michael, of course, had redeemed himself with her by wanting to settle down in Shepherd Valley. Now she wouldn't have to sacrifice Whitney's friendship.

She couldn't help but contrast the two men who had played such significant parts in Whitney's life. Cory Ross, responsible for so much destruction and pain in the lives of others, was dead, killed by his own hand that awful day on the mountain. He had turned the gun to his head shortly before the police reached him.

His death ended the investigation into the slayings of three young women, one of whom had been the niece of Michael's detective partner in Cincinnati. *And one of them could so easily have been Whitney,* she reminded herself uncomfortably.

As for Michael, she thought with a satisfied smile, hadn't he come around, though? He had made a total rededication of his life to Christ and, to hear Whitney tell it, was becoming so involved with various members of the community who needed help, he was getting downright *pushy.*

She didn't realize she'd chuckled out loud until Lyss elbowed her. Sobering, she sat up and scanned the auditorium with an appreciative eye, cherishing all of it—the families, the candlelight, the music, the poinsettias, the love . . . especially the love.

At the end of the service, after all the candles had been lighted and the last carol sung, Jennifer watched Daniel rise from the organ bench and make his way to the platform. The movement of his lips was scarcely visible as he counted off his steps until he reached the front.

Turning, he invited everyone to join hands as he led the choir and congregation in a musical benediction.

Then he prayed.

"Dear Lord and Father . . . let us join hearts as well as hands tonight. Bring us together as we've never been before, and help us to realize how greatly we are blessed to be standing here with those we love. For by the time Christmas comes again, some here tonight may no longer be with us. Indeed, we may never be together in quite this way again.

Tonight, like every other night you grant us, is a gift to be held gently, with great care, a gift to be cherished.

"And what an incredible gift it is, Lord, to be loved—by our husbands and our wives, our children and our parents, our sweethearts and our friends—so many different kinds of love, so many different ways you show your love for those you created.

"So before we leave this place tonight, Father, to go home to the trees and the gifts and the food and the laughter, to share the dreams and the memories that are so much a part of this precious time you've given us, help us to look at one another from the heart and really *see* each other . . . and then to say, 'I love you—you're a gift from God to me . . .'

"For that's the gift of Christmas, Father—your love for us and ours for one another. We thank you for the incredible pricelessness of it through your Son, Jesus Christ. And above all else this Christmas, teach us to *be* a people of love. Teach us to love one another . . . while we can . . . as you love us.

"In the name of Jesus Christ, the infant who came to be our Savior, our Lord, and our King . . .

"*Amen.*"